Bailey's Comet

BAILEY'S COMET

A SOURWOOD, TEXAS WESTERN

GARY GOLDSTEIN

THORNDIKE PRESS
A part of Gale, a Cengage Company

GALE
A Cengage Company

GALE
A Cengage Company

Thorndike Press, a part of Gale, a Cengage Company.

Thorndike Press® Large Print Hardcover Western.
The text of this Large Print edition is unabridged.
Other aspects of the book may vary from the original edition.
Set in 16 pt. Plantin.

**LIBRARY OF CONGRESS CIP DATA ON FILE.
CATALOGUING IN PUBLICATION FOR THIS BOOK
IS AVAILABLE FROM THE LIBRARY OF CONGRESS.**

ISBN-13: 978-1-4205-3702-4 (hardcover alk. paper)

Published in 2026 by arrangement with The John Talbot Agency, Inc.

Print Number: 1 Print Year: 2026
Printed in Mexico

"There's two ways of arguin' with a Texan.
Neither one works."

— Author unknown

"I plan on living forever. So far, so good."

— Author prefers to be unknown

10 BAILEY STREET
BAILEYVILLE, TEXAS

The Editors
Livermore and Beedle Publishing
26 Maiden Lane
New York City, New York
USA
August 10, 1945

Dear Sirs:
My name is Darris Bobby Ballard and I am 80 years old. But in the grand scheme of things, who I am is of no consequence, given the real story.

I take pen in hand today to complain about the recent publication of the book "Nightmare in Sourwood" by T. Chesney Ragsdale.

It is total hogwash and not worth the paper it is printed on.

Mr. Ragsdale was no more a glint in his mother's eye when Bailey's Comet came to Sourwood in 1874. His book is nothing but week-old corned beef hash, clearly cobbled together from newspaper and magazine pieces that were nothing but fabrications, then and now.

I know the Mr. Ragsdale's book is riddled with untruths because I was there, in Sourwood, when the world came crashing down.

I was all of eight years old at the time. Many, many others have claimed over the years that they remember the event but they are full of prairie oysters.

To the best of my knowledge, I am the only living soul from that time who remembers it vividly, almost as if it happened yesterday.

It has become my moral obligation then, to finally set the record straight once and for all. With the publication of "Nightmare in Sourwood," many have requested to interview me about the sheer terror of believing it was the end of the world. I refused all requests because it is not, nor has it ever been, something I care to relive.

However, it is all the falsehoods and out-and-out untruths culminating with Mr. Ragsdale's book (for which I paid three dollars and fifty cents) that have inspired me to write the true account — and I mean 100% true, not the second-or-third-or-fourth — or fifth-hand accounts that have cropped up over the years. (The manuscript was written with the help of my college-going great-grandson, Percy Hubert Ballard). It is included herewith.

It is my hope that Livermore and Beedle will print up my story and set the record straight for future generations. I am not looking for money, nor do I aspire to become a literary shining light.

I only wish for the truth to be known. To tell the real horror story that befell Sourwood, Texas, that fateful summer.

Because — as I have stated — I was there.

Please accept my gracious thanks in advance for your time and consideration. To that end, I remain

Sincerely yours,
Darris Bobby Ballard

Chapter 1

It was eight in the morning but the temperature was nudging its way up to 95 degrees.

"If you can't stand the heat, get out of Texas," was the common response when folks complained about the sweltering heat.

Most of the folks in the small town of Sourwood, Texas, however, were used to the searing climate. Today was a day pretty much like all the others.

Deputy Marshall William Thaddeus Bailey, all of twenty-four, kept the peace. He was liked by most of the folks in Sourwood, much like his late father, Braddock "Brad" Jacobus Bailey had been. A virulent strain of scarlet fever had taken Braddock Bailey to heaven eight years earlier, when his son William was sixteen. Braddock's wife, Maise, died a year later — some said from a broken heart.

The day he turned eighteen, William Bailey ran for deputy marshal and won handily, since no one else wanted the job.

That morning, he was having his breakfast at Miss Amelia Tuddy's Tasty Food Café — three eggs over easy, grits, biscuits and cream gravy, and bacon fresh from Wolfgang Dunderbeck's butcher shop. He was voraciously hungry — the night before had kept him hopping. A drunken brawl had broken out in the Saddle Sore Saloon between Alfie Futter and Herschel Copley over . . . well, no one could quite recall what they were fighting about. Something to do with a saloon gal from Fort Worth named Bootsie O'Dell. The fight would have ended right after Alfie smashed a chair over Herschel's noggin, putting him down.

Then Herschel's brother, Hiram, jumped into the battle, as did Futter's cousins Zeke and Zebulon. What had been an everyday argument spiraled into a free-for-all, fists flying, chairs smashed over heads.

Deputy Marshal William Bailey waded into the fray — all in a night's work — swinging his wooden club and smashing it into various ribs, clavicles, forearms, kneecaps, bellies, thighs, and a few groins. When the smoke cleared, seven men lay on the floor, clutching their wounded body parts in pain.

"Y'all go on home now, all of you," Bailey

shouted. "Dumb clucks."

The owner and bartender of the Saddle Sore, Wallace "Tubby" Nooner, was sweeping up the shattered glass, smashed chairs, and overturned poker table when Bailey stopped by later that morning.

"Everything all right, Tubs?" Bailey asked.

"As right as they'll ever be, I reckon," Tubby said. He shook his head sadly, looking at the wreckage, and said, "Sourwood. Where home is where the heart is. Heart attack, that is."

Across the street, barber Lomax Milligan was giving some guy a shave, asking, "Is it warmer in the country than it is in the summer? Or vice versa?" There was no correct answer but it kept potential blabbermouth customers quiet. The worst was Clarence Dowdy, who could start an argument in an empty room.

Next door was Chester Sturdley's Mercantile, providing provisions to the good folks of Sourwood. A sign on the window read "Canned peaches, three for 25 cents." They sold quickly but at a loss, so Sturdley raised the prices on everything else.

Welcome to Sourwood, Texas. Population 1,200. A nice peaceful town for the most part, and a fine place to raise up your brood.

Ask any citizen of Sourwood what the

folks do for fun and the answer is usually "Mind our own beeswax."

CHAPTER 2

"Yes, we'll gather by the river,
The beautiful, beautiful river;
Gather with the saints at the river
That flows by the throne of the Lord."

Wallis Asbury Pinkley, mayor of Sourwood, Texas, and town coroner when necessary, closed his hymnal and looked out on the good citizens of the town. They'd come to mourn the passing of Reverend Broadhurst, the preacher who'd been ministering to the spiritual, religious needs of the Lord's flock in the town for the last ten years.

Nobody was really certain of what caused Reverend Broadhurst's untimely demise — diphtheria, said some; others maintained it was influenza. Both were of considerable concern to those who'd been thrown into contact with him — because whichever it was, they were both contagious.

"Reverend Broadhurst was fond of saying,

'Hard work never killed anybody, but why take the chance?' And now —"

"And now the gophers are bringin' his mail!"

This came from the unmistakable voice of Fendall Harper, the town character. None of the mourners were particularly shocked — Fendall was always saying oddball stuff.

Miss Amelia Tuddy, who ran the café, gave Fendall an elbow in the ribs, and not gently. "Hush up, you doddering old fool," she said.

"Old?" Fendall asked. "Why I'll dance on your grave, you hash-slinging —"

"That's enough, Fendall," Deputy Marshal William Bailey said.

Kunkel gave Fendall an icy glare and went on, "So, in this, the year of our Lord, 18 and 74, we hereby lay to rest Reverend Hiram Broadhurst. And with that, I suggest we all bow our heads in devout prayer."

The mourners of Sourwood did just that. Mayor Pinkley opened his mouth to speak again, but no words came out. His face was the color of pemmican cheese and he was sweating like a stuck pig. He clutched his chest as his legs gave way as he tumbled head-first into the grave and fell face-down on top of Reverend Broadhurst's coffin.

There was a stunned silence until Fendall

Harper said, "Some coroner. Looks like he's his own best customer."

Deputy Marshal William Bailey made his way into the grave, as did the town sawbones. Doc Cutwater, who checked the mayor for a pulse, said to Bailey, "Help me turn him over."

They did. Pinkley's eyes were still wide open. Doc shook his head sadly as he gently closed them.

"Good lord," said an old woman. "Is he dead?"

"If he ain't," said Fendall Harper, "he's damn well doing a fine job of pretending."

Chapter 3

Sourwood, Texas
A few days later

Miss Amelia, clutching a tray covered with napkins, kicked open the door to the jailhouse. She was into her forties now but still looked pretty darn fine considering.

She put the tray down on the desk. Behind the desk sat Deputy Sheriff William Bailey. He lifted the napkin off the tray and gazed down at his lunch — a slab of something, singed around the edges — some would say burned. It was sort of grayish color that not even a healthy dollop of brown gravy could cover up.

Bailey asked, poking at it with a fork, "What kind of meat is this exactly, Amelia?"

She said, "You'll be better off if you eat it now and name it later."

There were also potatoes fried in what tasted like axle grease, snap peas–boiled too long and making them mushy, a couple of singed biscuits, hot coffee, and a piece of apple pie that looked older than Methuselah.

"Right," Bailey said.

"By the by, Billy," Miss Amelia said, "Old Fendall Harper is down at the Saddle Sore swiggin' rotgut straight from the bottle — and it sure as heck ain't making him any nicer."

"Fendall Harper," Bailey said, sounding a mite disgusted. Lunch would have to wait, not a bad thing actually. He stood and put on his gun belt and holster, which held an 1860 Colt Army revolver.

"Carrying on about ghosts in San Antonio and someone called La Llorona and Jesus coming to town on an old mule," Miss Amelia said with a weary wave of a hand.

"An *old* mule?" he asked, reaching into a desk drawer and pulling out his trusty blackjack. "Can't Jesus afford a new one?"

"You'll have to take that up with Fendall Harper," she said, but before she left, she added, "And you mind yourself, William Bailey — Fendall can be a real beast when he's liquored up. Don't let him kill you too much."

This much was true. Harper wasn't an outlaw or a hardcase, not violent really, at least when he was forking hay or mucking out horse droppings at Calvin Culpepper's stable. A comedown for a former Texas Ranger who'd never touched a drop until he was retired. That was when he started drowning his sorrows in whiskey.

Bailey thought to himself, well, things have been kind of quiet in Sourwood lately — the most exciting thing that happened recently was when Amos Helmer brought to town an egg from his farm that had three yolks in it. It was all the talk in Sourwood for weeks.

Thus far, after two years on the job of keeping the peace and maintaining law and order in Sourwood, that special occasion had yet to show itself. No, things were quiet. Texas was governed by a series of provisional governors as the state went through Reconstruction, a pretty-sounding word for ridding the land of carpetbaggers. The Texas Rangers had the Comanche all balled up; closer to Sourwood, Federals were chasing outlaws. A year-long drought was making life rotten for folks in the territory.

Chapter 4

Fendall Harper was standing on a poker table, cards and silver coins scattered all over the floor, a bottle of rotgut clenched in his fist. He bellowed, "A legend with deep roots in Mexican folklore, La Llorona, the Weeping Woman was a Mex woman American folklore mourning her children shc drowned in a jealous rage after discovering her husband was unfaithful to her. She is said to wander rivers and lakes at night, wracked with guilt. She drowned herself as well but couldn't enter the spirit life, forced into purgatory to roam between the winds for eternity. Her mournful wails echoed through the darkness, scaring the bejesus out of the locals! Along the Rio Grande and in San Antonio, lotta older Texans grew up with this story, turning La Llorona into a folklore but my hand to God, I saw her spirit clear as day."

There were several snorts of disbelief but

Fendall ignored them, saying, "Then late one night I was crossing the Brazos River Bridge when La Llorona kind of floated out of nowhere and said to me, 'Oh my children, where am I to take you?'

"I won't deny it — I was scared right down to my socks. All I could think to say was, 'How can I help you, missy?'

" 'My children, you must help me find my children,' La Llorona pleaded. I said to her, I cannot help — it is beyond my power as a human being.

"She said, 'Then take a long bath, get your hair cut and have yourself a shave — you look like you just crawled out of a slop bucket.' And she vanished right back into the chilly night air."

"Poppycock," someone blurted.

Fendall didn't like that too much. He hopped off the poker table and started throwing anything within reach — bottles, glasses, even chairs that shattered all over the place. Fendall drew his pistol and started firing at the ceiling.

"I'll show you poppycock!" he bellowed.

Fendall flung an empty bottle across the room, missing Bailey by about an inch as he stepped through the batwing doors.

Tubby Nooner was crouching behind the bar. Now huddled in all corners were poker players and some barflies. No one was safe when Fendall Harper was snockered.

The sheriff stepped inside the Saddle Sore.

Bailey asked Tubby Nooner, "How long has he been like this?"

Nooner, poking his head up from beyond the bar, said, "Right after he sucked up that second bottle of hooch."

Bailey said, "I've seen Fendall drunker than a boiled owl — I suppose he shared the La Llorona story?"

Nooner said, "Yeah, for the millionth time."

Fendall's next shot hit a portrait of a scantily clad songbird, Miss Aggie March, who played before the crowned heads in Europe, all of whom wanted to marry her. She was the fantasy of every red-blooded man in the west — her picture hung in dozens of watering holes.

Even three sheets in the wind, Fendall Harper was a damn good shot — the bullet hit Miss Aggie March right in the center of her forehead. As Sourwood's former deputy, serving under Bill Bailey's late father, he'd also been the town marshal.

Bailey asked, "You still got that sledge-hammer, Lomax?"

Nooner pulled out the sledgehammer he kept behind the bar and handed it to Bailey, saying, "A barkeep's best friend."

"Give me a bottle, too."

Nooner gave Baily a bottle of his cheapest hooch — Old Panther. Bailey waited till Harper fired the last of the bullets in his pistol until all he got were dry clicks when he pulled the trigger.

Before Fendall could reload, Bailey came out from behind the bar, strolled over to where the drunkard, sitting cross-legged on the poker table now, was trying to get the bullet-less gun to fire. Bailey up-ended the table and sent Harper flying backwards. He flapped his arms like a sparrow, crossed his eyes almost comically, and toppled to the floor.

There was a pail full of dirty water with a mop in it. Bailey grabbed it.

"Got something on your mind do you, Fendall?" Bailey asked.

"Well yes," Fendall said drunkenly. "I see three of you, Billy, but I happen to know there's only one you . . . unless you got yourself two twin brothers."

"No, just me," Bailey said, and emptied the bucket on Fendall Harper's noggin.

Harper sputtered back to consciousness and looked up at Bailey. "What in the blue blazes!" he sputtered.

"Can you stand up, Fendall?" Bailey asked.

"Damn right I can," Harper said, still slurring his words. "And when I do, I'm gonna knock you into the middle of next week."

He managed to get to his feet for about two seconds, then collapsed ass down. He tried again with similar results.

"Judgment Day, that's what's coming for us all," Harper said, and passed out cold. Bailey threw the rest of the water on him but Harper didn't stir."

"I think you got him, Billy," Nooner said.

"I've seen Fendall cockeyed drunk before," Bailey said, "but nothing like this."

"I don't envy him," Nooner said. "When he comes to, his head is gonna throb like a Chinese gong."

"Let's get him back to the jail till he sleeps it off," Bailey said. "Help me get him up."

Together, each man took an arm and lifted Harper, still out cold, to his feet. They got two steps toward the swinging bar room doors when Nooner's knees buckled and all three of them tumbled to the floor.

"Why the hell did you let him get so stinking drunk, Tubby?" Bailey asked.

"A wise man once said 'Live in harmony with the land, and it will live in harmony with you.' "

"And just what the hell is that supposed to mean?"

"I dunno." Nooner shrugged. "It just sounded good."

This time, each of them took a leg, pulled Harper outside and dragged him down the street to the jailhouse. It was a few minutes after noon and already the heat was brutal. Bailey and Nooner stopped pulling, let loose Harper's legs, and wiped the sweat off their brows.

Harper came to, goggle-eyed as he looked up at the sky. He pointed to the heavens, saying "There it is! I knew I seen it."

Bailey and Nooner looked up simultaneously into a cloudless, sun-drenched Texas sky. They saw nothing but blue. Bailey blinked a few times to clear his vision — sweat was running into his eyes — and briefly glimpsed a yellow dot. Then it was gone.

"I see it now," Nooner said. "Looks like a mess of mustard."

Bailey said, "That's a star. Lots of 'em out there I hear tell."

"A star, my sweet dimpled behind," Harper said. "Stars don't shine during the day."

"Sometimes they do," Nooner said. "I read in a newspaper once that said big chunks of stars are floating around the heavens. Maybe that's what it is, a chunk of star."

Fendall said, "Chunk, chunk, chunk," and passed out again.

Nooner shook his head sadly as he looked down on an inebriated and once agin unconscious Fendall Harper. "Judgment Day?" Nooner said.

"Yes, with mustard," Bailey said.

"With mustard," Nooner said.

Fendall Harper was snoring contentedly in the Sourwood jail. It was going on suppertime so he'd probably be hungry when he awakened.

Bailey left the cell door unlocked. Harper wasn't going anywhere, at least not until he was fed. Bailey headed out to Amelia's Tasty Food Café to fetch the day's special: pork chops that were 90% fat, 10% pork, and coffee. "Take the whole pot," Amelia told him. "He's gonna need it."

As a rule, Bailey did not take his meals at Amelia's Tasty Food Café, about which a whiskey drummer once commented, "At Amelia's, the food is so bad people pray *after* they eat."

No, Bailey took his meals at Mrs. Liddiflower Gribble's boarding house, where supper didn't come right back up moments after it went down. There were worse places for a man to hang his hat. Chicken croquettes this evening, she had promised. Bailey's belly rumbled. He never quite got around to eating the lunch from Amelia's.

Bailey strolled down Main Street, greeting the townsfolk. Sourwood's merchants were closing up shop for the day. Later, he'd walk over to visit with Miss Agnes Jean Willoughby, where she lived in a clapboard house with her Aunt Tinky. Agnes Jean worked for Chester Sturdley, of the Sourwood Mercantile. She and Bailey had been courting for most of their lives, and the subject of marriage was a subject Agnes Jean was bringing up more and more. She was for certain the prettiest gal in Sourwood ("which ain't hard," Miss Amelia said. "We only got a couple be of much interest to anyone") and the eligible men in town — and some who weren't — swarmed around her.

It was a beautiful dusk, cooling off after the day's oppressive heat. The moon was rising and Bailey was in a good mood. Maybe tonight he'd broach the subject of wedded bliss for —

He stopped abruptly and looked up at the darkening sky. Damn if he didn't notice that yellow dot, the same one Fendall Harper had been drunkenly ranting about. It burned brighter than the stars . . . and somehow now it looked slightly bigger in the night sky than before.

Bailey took Fendall's dinner to the jail and thought no more about it.

Chapter 5

Dinwiddie, Texas

"If there's one thing I hate, it's having to repeat myself."

Dexter "Dex" McGoon cocked his Colt .45 revolver through the cage's iron bars and pressed the end of the barrel flat on the teller's nose. The teller, who looked all of eighteen and 145 pounds soaking wet, looked appropriately terrified. His name pin said "Mervin Gladstone."

"I'll ask you again," McGoon said. "What is the combination for the safe, Mr. Gladstone?"

The teller made a somewhat pathetic attempt at speech but he couldn't stop quaking with fear. Sweat dribbled down his forehead. Dexter McGoon fired a shot a few inches over Gladstone's head, where it smashed into the clock. Gladstone felt his knees turn to water and he fought to keep from fainting dead away.

It being almost three p.m., the Dinwiddie Merchant and Trust Bank was about to close up shop; the only ones present were Gladstone, Ollie Perkins, the bookkeeper, and Mrs. Alma Honeywell, the widow of Cornelius, a farmer who got kicked in the head by a mule. Wasn't the kick that got him dead, though — he stumbled backwards from the force of the kick and fell on a pitchfork. Alma wanted to get him a nice headstone. For that she needed to withdraw some bank money. It was $300.

Alma said, "Leave the boy alone, you fool. Mr. Dinwiddie's the only one who knows the combination and he's out of town till next week."

"Is he askin' you, lady?" This from Stuffy Stan McElroy, one of McGoon's kill-crazy weasels. Stuffy was allergic to just about everything. He sneezed, then aimed his pistol at the Widow Honeywell and fired. The bullet struck her in the left eye. She looked stunned momentarily, then collapsed

"Good Lord," Gladstone said, his eyes almost popping out of his head.

"You half-wit," McGoon said to Stuffy. "Now we're gonna have every man in town with a gun trying to fill us full of lead." To another of his gang, Mossy Grandstaff, he said, "Give me the dynamite. We're gonna blow this safe to high heaven."

Outside the bank, minding the horses and keeping watch for the law, another of McGoon's gang, Ethan Kunkle spotted some movement on the other side of the street and then a glint from a gun barrel. To let his partners know they were expecting company, he burst through the door of the bank moments after McGoon lit the fuse. The stick of dynamite detonated with a brain-scrambling roar that shattered the windows and sent debris flying, included half a dozen quill pens that became airborne from the force of the blast and flew into the face of Mossy Grandstaff, making him look insanely like a shedding porcupine. While the others were crouched low in a corner, Kunkle was blown backwards from the force of the blast and into the street, courtesy of a large chunk of window glass that became embedded in his chest.

But the dynamite did its job. The safe blew open.

"That should attract some unwanted attention," McGoon said, his ears still ringing. Stuffy Stan was pulling quill pens from his face. McGoon said to Sneed Hearn, a loyal member of the McGoon band of cutthroats, "Go on out there and have a confab with the welcoming committee while we grab the booty." He did as ordered, and the exchange of gunfire started at once.

When the smoke cleared, McGoon looked inside. The safe was empty save for a few scattered paper bills and coins. McGoon scooped up the little pile and announced in disgust, "Thirty-three dollars. Thirty-three egg-sucking dollars!"

Stuffy Stan turned to Gladstone, who was crouched behind the manager's desk. Stuffy said, "Why didn't you tell us the safe was empty?"

Gladstone said, "You didn't ask me."

Stuffy Sam pointed his pistol at Gladstone and then sneezed twice — he was allergic to something around here.

"Bless you," Gladstone said.

"Thank you," Stuffy said, and shot the bank clerk twice in the face, taking a good chunk of Gladstone's skull along with it.

"What the hell you do that for?" McGoon said angrily, "We're thieves, not savages."

"Can't we be both?" Stuffy said, and sneezed again. No one, however, said, "bless you" this time.

"Well, put your bloodlust away, for corn's sake!"

Stuffy holstered his pistol and went for his Winchester. He pushed through what was left of the bank's door.

Stuffy turned his gunsights on shots coming from the mercantile and next door at the livery stable. Stuffy aimed, fired, and dropped one do-gooder like a rock. He dropped another one with a perfectly aimed shot right above the left eye. The other folks in the street ran for cover in all directions; Stuffy kept firing, not caring who he hit.

In the chaotic confusion, McGoon, Hearn, and Grandstaff slipped out of the bank and hopped onto their horses.

Mossy Grandstaff, also mounting up, said, "What about Kunkle?"

"What about him?" McGoon said, putting spurs to flanks.

"We gonna leave him there?" Mossy asked.

"Stay with him if you're so damn worried," McGoon said. "But don't expect much in the way of conversation."

"They'll be forming a posse for us," Stuffy said.

"It'll take these neck-bowed morons an hour at least to get a posse together," McGoon said. "And by then they won't see our coattails for the dust."

Thirty-three dollars, McGoon thought, utterly disgusted. A bunch of folks dead for thirty-three lousy stinking dollars.

There had to be an easier way to make a

living. Thievery just didn't pay the way it once did.

Chapter 6

Sourwood, Texas

Lomax Milligan started digging a hole in the middle of his shop at five A.M. that morning. He'd chopped through the wooden floorboards to the ground below and by eight A.M., the hole was about a foot deep — Texas soil was rocky and dry, making the digging an arduous process. But dig he did.

Lomax Milligan was the only barber in Sourwood. In addition to haircuts, his shop offered hot baths and even boot repair. Milligan was a short, chubby man who could make conversation on almost any topic, be it politics ("President Useless Grant enjoys stewed prunes for lunch"), love ("love can take flight — usually right out the window"), or even science ("Did you know the magpie is the only bird that sees itself in a mirror?"). Lomax Milligan was also most of the way to balding, normally a hazard of his profession but folks didn't care — Lomax gave a good haircut.

Bailey was shielding his eyes from the blazing sun, on his way to Miss Amelia's café for coffee and maybe a slab of cherry pie. That yellow star was still up there — it seemed bigger now but that might have been his imagination. What grabbed his attention was the sight of Lomax Milligan single-mindedly destroying his barber shop. He was making progress — a mound of freshly dug dirt was now piled three feet high. Milligan was standing in the hole, shovel in hand — he was visible only from the chest up. His bald pate was glistened with sweat.

"Morning, Lomax," Bailey said.

The barber grunted something unintelligible. He was usually bright and chipper in the morning.

"Wanna tell me what you're up to, Lomax?"

"Digging a hole," he snapped. "What in blazes does it look like I'm doing?"

"It looks like you're digging a hole," Bailey said. "So I guess my next question is, *why* are you digging a hole in your floor?"

"China," Milligan said, as if that answered it.

"China?"

"I'm digging my way to China," Milligan said. "It's been said that if you dig deep enough, you can be in China."

"What's in China that we don't have in Sourwood?" Bailey asked.

"Chinese people," Milligan said, heaving a shovelful of dirt upward, where it landed squarely in Bailey's face. He brushed it out of his eyes, then noticed Milligan's spittoon sitting on the barber chair above the mountain of earth. Milligan usually kept it by the door.

"Taking your spittoon, are you?"

Milligan said, "Damn right. I paid thirty dollars for that thing, ain't leaving it here. And the China people mightn't have any."

"You can't really dig down to China, Lomax. That's just a crazy legend. What's so special about China anyway?"

"It ain't Texas," Lomax said. "And there ain't no yellow ball in the sky there. So go ahead and stay here in Sourwood and don't blame me when the Good Lord hurls bolts of fire down on your heads." He wiped his brow with a hanky and asked Bailey, "Wanna come with me? Take turns digging and such."

"Not for all the tea in China," Bailey said.

"It's your funeral, Billy," Milligan said.

He had no choice but to grab Milligan by

the collar and drag him out of the hole, still clutching the shovel. "Enough, Lomax, unless you want to dig your way to China from the inside of a jail cell."

Milligan's face turned red, flushed with anger. He swung the shovel at Bailey's noggin — who ducked just in time so the tool only knocked his hat off. Half a second less and Milligan would have split Bailey's skull.

Bailey snatched the shovel from Milligan's hands. "Give me that," he said. He grabbed Milligan by the collar and marched him off to jail.

"It's my barbershop, Billy," Milligan said, "and I'm well within my rights as a citizen to —"

"You wanna go to China, Lomax," Bailey said, wondering what had gotten into Milligan, normally a sane, rational man, "take a slow boat like everyone else."

After locking Milligan in a cell — Fendall was still occupying the other one — Bailey walked into Amelia's café and said, "Coffee and a piece of blueberry pie, Amelia."

"Ain't got no blueberry pie," Amelia hollered from the kitchen, where she was yelling at the Mexican cook, Carlos Ninni. "You'll eat what I got."

"Fine," Bailey said. Arguing with Amelia

was pointless.

Amelia's café was unusually quiet for what was the busy breakfast hour. Two hands from Oraville Kunz's Twisted Oak Ranch were finishing up breakfast at a table in the back. Sitting alone at a table staring morosely at a cup of coffee and a plate of untouched ham and eggs was Doc Cutwater. He'd brought William Bailey into this world twenty-four years earlier.

"Mind if I join you, Doc?" Bailey asked.

"By all means, William," Doc said. "Though I'm not the best company right now."

Bailey sat. Amelia came out with a cup of coffee and a slice of pie — what kind of pie was anyone's guess.

Amelia looked down at Doc Cutwater's uneaten ham and eggs. "Got here just in time, Billy," she said, plopping the pie on the table. "If it ain't food Doc Cutwater is wanting, maybe it's conversation."

She disappeared back into the kitchen. Bailey said, "You all right there, Doc? You look lower than a snake's toes."

And he did. Doc Cutwater looked tired — exhausted actually, and older than his sixty-one years.

"I'm worried, William," Doc said. "No, make that very worried."

"Why?"

"Don't forget about Hortense Primm," Amelia yelled from the kitchen.

"What about Hortense Primm?" Bailey asked.

Doc said, "She came screaming into my office yesterday, saying a couple of prairie rats were in her house trying to take her virginity."

"She's been doing that for years," Bailey said. "Why didn't you send for me?"

"Everybody in town knows Hortense Primm is a few years over ninety," Amelia hollered. "Hell, iffen she hasn't surrendered her maidenhead yet, somehow I 'spect she never will."

"Been seeing some very unusual behavior in Sourwood lately," Doc said.

Bailey said, "Very." He kept thinking about Milligan digging a hole in the floor of his barber shop.

Doc said, "Farmer Nob Helmer came by my office this morning. Darn chickens are off their feed, Nob said. And his cows stopped giving milk. And it isn't just Nob Helmer, either. Yesterday, Arthur Beanstock said he's got the same problem."

Though his practice was limited to human beings, the townsfolk often went to Doc Cutwater with all kinds of problems, not all of them health related.

Bailey nodded and said, "Charlotte Dalrymple came by the jail yesterday, wanted me to form a search party for her sister, Petunia Mae, who never came home for apple picking."

Doc said, "Petunia Mae? She's been dead for ten years."

Bailey nodded. "I also found Lomax Milligan trying to dig his way to China," he said.

Doc said, "Something's ailing this town. I don't know much about science, William, but nothing in medical school prepared me for this."

Amelia yelled from the kitchen. "Oh hell, dying is easy in Texas."

Doc yelled back, "You would know, Amelia. You do your killing with a frying pan and ten pounds of lard." To Bailey, he said, "Let's go see how Hortense Primm is feeling."

"Is Miss Primm under arrest?"

Agnes Jean stood in the doorway of Hortense Primm's frame house and shot Bailey a withering look.

Damn, he reminded himself for the tenth time that day, but she was astonishingly beautiful. Her hair was a rich, dark brown that cascaded down her shoulders in soft waves, her skin was smooth and flawless, with a hint of color in her cheeks. Her eyes were a deep, mesmerizing green that seemed to sparkle in the dim lantern light. Bailey found it impossible not to gaze at her. As did virtually all the men in Sourwood and beyond.

Bailey and Doc could hear Hortense Primm inside the house carrying on about . . . something.

"And the early wheel gets the worm, the squeaky bird gets the grease," she was saying. "If a horse can smell water, why are cucumbers so costly . . . ?"

Doc eased Agnes Jean aside and went into the house. Bailey started to follow when she grabbed his arm.

"Where were *you* last night, William Bailey?" she asked. "I baked you a great big rhubarb pie, then waited and waited but saw neither hide nor hair of you."

Even angry, she was beautiful.

"We got some problems in Sourwood," Bailey said, and went on in.

In the bedroom, Doc reached into his bag and pulled out a green bottle with a cork in it.

"You get out of my home now, Black Ear Cicero! You rustled forty head of cattle from

Amos Wheeler's ranch last week . . ."

"Black Ear Cicero was killed by the Texas Rangers twenty years ago, Hortense," Doc said.

Doc pulled a battered spoon from his bag and poured some brown syrup into it. "Now take this. Make you feel better."

Miss Primm waved him away, saying, "You stay away from me, you . . . you *man*! Nothing but rough, hairy beasts who only want one thing from a lady!" She was almost screaming now so Doc used the opportunity to shove the spoonful of medicine into her mouth.

"Now swallow," he instructed. He filled the spoon again.

Miss Primm spat out the offering and screeched, "You got any notion to gettin' biblical with me, mister, you got another thing —"

Doc shoved the spoon into her mouth and then pinched her nostrils shut. "Let's try it again, Hortense." This time, she downed the foul tasting medicine. Doc said, "Let's try one more." He poured more syrup into the spoon. Miss Primm didn't make a fuss this time. In fact, she calmed down some and sang, "Cabbages and onions, can't stand ice cream cones . . . I like bananas because they have no bones . . ."

Within minutes, Hortense Primm was out, snoring contentedly.

"What kind of medicine is that?" Agnes Jean asked.

"Silk Hat Harry's Magic Humor Cure," Doc said. "Remember when that snake oil peddler passed through Sourwood last year?"

"Sure," Bailey said. "He told Mert Newton his humor cure would make his piles go away and when it didn't, we ran him out of town."

"Not before I purchased a bottle of his 'magic' elixir," Doc said. "I wanted to see for myself what Silk Hat Harry was putting into the stuff. From what I could tell, it's Epsom salts, burnt sugar, licorice powder, laudanum, and enough grain alcohol to knock out a buffalo."

"Poor Miss Primm," Agnes Jean said.

"Walk the lady home, William," Doc said. "and both you get yourselves some rest. Something tells me you're gonna need it."

CHAPTER 7

Though they'd known each other since childhood and it was assumed by everyone in Sourwood that William Bailey and Agnes Jean Willoughby were engaged to be betrothed — or as Agnes Jean claimed, "Engaged to be engaged." Billy was still shy about holding her hand as they walked to where Agnes Jean lived with her spinster aunt, Miss Tinky Grissel.

When they reached the house — which needed a lot of fixing, a man's touch some might say — and sat down on the porch swing. The breeze from the north had cooled things down somewhat. Bailey put his arm around her but went no further. Agnes Jean set the romantic rules. Bailey dutifully followed them. He also had no doubt that eagle-eyed Aunt Tinky was likely lurking in the shadows by the window, watching Bailey's every move.

"I need to ask you something, Billy,"

she said.

"I'm right here, Aggie."

"Are you ever going to propose?" she said. "I love you, Billy, but I can't wait any longer. I won't."

"Aggie —"

"Maybe you're waiting for someone better to come along," Agnes Jean said. "Someone prettier . . ."

"In Sourwood?" He almost said, "Talk about roses on the dung heap," but wisely held his tongue.

"Or someone . . . younger," she said.

"Younger? We're the same age," Bailey said.

There was a pause when Agnes Jean said, "I wasn't going to say anything, but Royal Briggs asked me to marry him."

"Royal Briggs? That ignorant slob? He's so dumb, he'd climb over a glass wall to see what's on the other side. If stupidity was a crime, Royal would be serving a life sentence."

"He's a nice young man," Agnes Jean said, "and a beautiful person on the inside. That's what matters."

"And those buck teeth," Bailey said. "Good Lord, he could eat a tomato through barbed wire and not spill a drop."

She said, "Dallas Horatio Paroo would

also like to marry me," she said.

Bailey snorted. "Fat Dal? Are you kidding? The man weighs over three hundred pounds. Hell, his shadow alone weighs fifty pounds. When he comes into a room, he sits next to *everybody.*"

"If you really and truly love me, William Thaddeus Bailey," Agnes Jean said, "you will ask me to marry you right here and now or else, my hand to God, I'll marry Royal Briggs or Fat Dal — I mean, Dallas Horatio Paroo, fat and all."

"Does anyone in your family suffer from insanity?" he asked.

"Just Aunt Tinky," Agnes Jean said. "And she enjoys every minute of it."

There was no getting out of it now, Bailey knew. Once Agnes Jean made up her mind, it was made up forever. She'd never actually marry Royal Briggs or Fat Dal, but Bailey gave her credit for trying to make him jealous — and to that end, those two were, sadly, about the best Sourwood had to offer for jealousy purposes.

As for other women, most of them in Sourwood were so homely you could throw one in a lake and skim ugly for a month.

Bailey knew it was time to fish or cut bait. He got down on one knee and said, "Agnes Jean, will you mar—"

"What are you doing, Billy?"

"I think I was proposing," he said. His bended knee landed on a rusty nail poking out of the front porch floor. He grunted in pain, thinking, *the things we do for love.*

"You can't propose till you ask Aunt Tinky for her blessing."

"Aunt Tinky?" Baily said, flustered as all get-out. "You're supposed to ask the father!"

"In case you hadn't noticed," Agnes Jean said, "my mother and father are deceased."

It was always better not to argue with Agnes Jean. "With women," he remembered some old-timer saying at the saloon, "even when you win the argument, you still lose. When you're right, you're still wrong."

Truer words, Bailey mused.

"Listen, Aggie —" Bailey began.

"Shut up and kiss me, dumbbell."

Bailey needed no further coaxing. He wrapped her in his arms and planted his lips firmly on hers. She responded in kind, kissing him back with more affection than usual.

In between kisses, his hand found her left bosom and he gave it a gentle squeeze. She didn't protest — Billy had melon-squeezed her in the past, and Agnes Jean understood the lusts of men. It was when his hand slid up her dress — this was a new maneuver —

and rested it on her corset. He was getting pretty excited.

Agnes Jean said, "What do you think you're doing, Billy?"

Is there a right answer to that, he wondered. He said, "Well, I —"

"I *know* what you're doing, Billy, and *you* know what you're trying to do but we agreed — nothing more than kissing until our wedding night."

"Does this mean you'll marry me?" Billy asked.

"Yes, Billy," she said. "I've loved you since the first time I set eyes on you, when we were knee-high to grasshoppers."

"What about Fat Dal Paroo?"

"We'll send him a nice fruitcake every Christmas," she said.

"Better be a big one," he said.

It was at that moment that they heard the sweet, dulcet tones of Aunt Tinky calling from the front door, "Get in the house now, Agnes Jean, or there'll be hell to pay." To Bailey she said, "Come around again, Bailey, and I'll blow your butt off."

The front door slammed shut. Bailey asked, "Why does she hate me so much?"

"She hates any man who can take me away from her. I'm all she has."

"You're all she deserves."

■ ■ ■ ■

"Hello, the camp!" came the voice from the darkness.

Axel Gallagher looked up from the campfire where he had coffee brewing. He was sitting on a tree stump. He grabbed his Henry and pointed it in the general direction the voice had come from.

"Come out and show yourself," Gallagher said.

Out of the gloom came a figure wearing a heavy black greatcoat and a black low top hat. As he came closer to the light, Gallagher made him for a man in his thirties. The man stepped a little closer to the fire until Gallagher said, "That's far enough, stranger. State your business."

The man in black said, "The Reverend Thornton Goodrich of the Methodist Episcopal Church in Abilene. At your service, sir. And who might you be, brother?"

"Name's Gallagher, Axel Gallagher, from down Sourwood way," he said. "Had me some business down San Saba way, now I'm heading home."

"Sourwood," Goodrich said. "I'm sure it's a very fine place to live."

Gallagher said, "Fair to middlin'."

"And how far is Sourwood from here, Mr. Gallagher?"

"A day's ride, maybe two if the weather ain't cooperatin'," he said. "What's that you're holding in your hand?"

"Why, the Good Book, sir, of course," Goodrich said. "The Gospel, the words every God-fearing man and woman should live by. As a servant of the Lord, the Good Book guides me to saving souls."

"You one of them saddlebag preachers?" Gallagher asked.

"We prefer to be known as circuit riders," Goodrich said. "We minister to settlers and organize congregations. Those too small to have their own houses of worship. They come to hear the word of the Lord so those who are troubled with unclean spirits are healed."

"I ain't the church-going type," Gallagher said. "All them preachers talk about are hell and damnation. Trust me, as a married man, I know all about hell and damnation."

"We are only strangers and sojourners in this life," Goodrich said. "Our citizenship is in Heaven."

"I ain't quite ready for that kind of citizenship," Gallagher said. "You wanna sojourn over here to the fire and have a cup of coffee?"

"I would be very grateful," Goodrich said.

"It ain't the best coffee you'll find," Gallagher said, filling a cup and handing it to Goodrich, "but it's the only coffee you'll find around here."

"Perish the thought," Goodrich said.

He flung the boiling hot coffee in Gallagher's face. Gallagher screamed out in agony as Goodrich produced a very long knife from under his greatcoat and plunged it into Gallagher's belly. Gallagher looked shocked momentarily, then grabbed Goodrich's wrist to stop the thrusting but it was too late. After a few futile tugs he fell over and croaked, — "Some rotten servant of the Lord you are," — and died.

"We all have our weaknesses, Mr. Gallagher," Goodrich said. He picked up Gallagher's Henry. "I could use me a good rifle." He rummaged through Gallagher's belongings and found a Colt 1851 Navy Revolver. "Could use me a good pistol, too."

He slapped Gallagher's horse on the rump and sent him galloping off. Goodrich mounted his horse, saying, "Sourwood, Texas. Sounds like a town I'd like to see."

CHAPTER 8

"Well, it's about time."

Aunt Tinky didn't even look up from her knitting. There she sat, next to the fireplace where a burning log crackled along to the clicking sounds of Aunt Tinky's knitting needles.

"Hello, Miss Tinky," Bailey said. "Hope you're well this evening."

"I don't see where it's any of your business," Aunt Tinky said.

Bailey sighed. Aunt Tinky never changed — she made no attempt to hide her dislike of him, despite the fact that he and her niece had been childhood sweethearts. But then, Aunt Tinky disliked everybody in Sourwood, and, quite possibly, the world.

At only forty years old, Aunt Tinky seemed to be in a furious trotting race toward old age-dom. Her hair was slate gray, tied in a severe bun. Her black, shapeless dress went straight down to her leather button shoes.

In the dim light, one could see where she had once been a pretty lady but now her face was etched in an ill-tempered, permanent scowl.

"Sorry, Aunt Tinky," Agnes Jean said. "Time just got away from us —"

"You go on upstairs and get to bed, Agnes Jean," Aunt Tinky said, and her tone indicated she would brook no protest. Agnes Jean was considered a grown-up in the outside world, but under Aunt Tinky's domineering thumb, she reverted almost to childhood.

"Goodnight, Billy," Agnes Jean said, and dutifully trotted up the stairs. There would be no kissing her goodnight, not with Terrible Tinky, as some townsfolk called her, sitting ten feet away.

"G'night, Aggie," Bailey said, and, putting his hat on, turned to leave. "And goodnight, Miss Tink—"

"Where do you think you're going?" Aunt Tinky asked.

"Home?" This was not, he knew, the best time to be asking Aunt Tinky for Aggie's hand in marriage. If ever there *was* a good time.

"Where do you get the nerve bringing my niece home at this hour?"

"It's only eight o'clock, Miss Tinky,"

Bailey said.

"Don't sass me, boy," Aunt Tinky said, "or I'll whale the tar out of you." She was knitting furiously now. Whatever she was creating, it was big enough to keep an elephant warm.

Bailey had had enough. Maybe Agnes Jean was afraid of her, but he wasn't. She'd been treating him like a mud and mustard sandwich for years. Enough was enough already.

"You don't like me very much, do you, Miss Tinky?"

"No more or no less than any other man I've ever met," she said.

This wasn't completely true — there had been a man once upon a time, or so Agnes Jean claimed, but she knew little else.

"You aim to marry my Agnes Jean, don't you, boy?"

Bailey nodded — words seemed pointless.

"That's not going to happen," she said. "I'll not have my niece marrying a lawman and worrying about whether her husband will be coming through the door or lying dead in the street with an outlaw's bullet in his brain."

Temper, Bailey reminded himself. *Temper.*

"You know, Miss Tinky," Bailey said, "I'm not so sure I want to be marrying into this family if you're part of the deal."

With that, he spun on his heels and walked out of the house. Then, naturally, came all the things he *should* have said in response but thought of them too late: "Ah, shut that hole in your face," or "You could make an onion cry," or "If I gave you a penny for your thoughts, I'd want change back."

But he had said none of these. He loved Agnes Jean much more than he despised her Aunt Tinky. He took two steps in the direction of the boardinghouse he called home when a good sized rock, still smoking, landed at his feet. He hopped backward in surprise, getting his legs all tangled, and fell flat on his rump with a jarring thud. He felt the pain in his teeth.

He looked up. Was someone throwing rocks at him from a rooftop? Probably that little rat dropping Amos McElroy, twelve-year old son of an even bigger rat dropping, Harlan McElroy.

But somehow, Bailey knew it wasn't Amos McElroy — not this time anyway. He looked up to the heavens. The red ball was still there, next to the moon.

Thing was, though, it was a little bigger now.

He returned to Miss Liddi's boarding

house, home sweet home. Miss Liddi almost thought of Billy Bailey as her own son. She had left a plate of sugar cookies and a glass of milk for him in the kitchen. If nothing else, her Billy was too thin. Boy plumb forgot to eat sometimes. Just like his daddy.

Matilda Gallagher said, "My Axel never came home."

Bailey asked, "When?"

Matilda, puzzled, said, "When what? When did he not come home?"

Matilda was a very attractive woman, easily fifteen years younger than her husband. No one in Sourwood could understand why she married Axel. There were also rumors that Wilbur Freeley, the blacksmith, was seen leaving the Gallagher ranch in the early hours of the morning in Axel's absence.

Matilda was holding back tears, and her nose was runny. Bailey gave her his handkerchief. She took it and wiped her teary eyes, then put it to her nose and gave it a healthy blow. She handed it back to him but Bailey said, "Keep it." Then he said, "Well, when did he leave?"

"Leave where?"

"When did he leave to go wherever it was he went?" Bailey asked.

Matilda looked puzzled for a moment and

said, "You mean when did he leave and not come back?"

"No," Bailey said. "What day did he leave home?"

"Four days ago, Sunday," she said.

Now we're getting somewhere, he mused. "And when did he say he was coming back?"

"He *didn't* come back," she said. "That's why I'm here."

From the jail cell, Fendall Harper — who'd been sleeping one off — said, "For corn's sake, Matilda, where the hell did Axel *go*?" He murmured to himself, "Lady ought to have her brains counted."

"To San Saba," Miss Matilda said, and the sobs started up again. "To see about buying a few head of cattle."

"Thank you," Fendall said, and tried to go back to sleep.

"Then it's safe to assume he'll come back by the same route," Bailey said. "I'll go look for him today. Maybe he got lost or something."

"Axel was born and raised in these parts," Miss Matilda said. "He knows it like the back of my hand."

Bailey let that one go. "Now, Miss Matilda," he said, "why don't you go over to

Miss Amelia's and get yourself a nice cup of tea?"

She said, "I don't like tea."

"Coffee then," Bailey said.

"I don't like coffee."

"Milk?" Bailey tried.

"Matilda, just tell Miss Amelia you want the special — three fingers of whiskey from the bottle she keeps hidden from the cook, Ninni."

"Fine," Miss Matilda said, "but can you find that husband of mine, please? If he doesn't want to come, so be it — be the happiest day of my life — just ask him where he keeps all his money. We got bills to pay."

Fendall said, "How touching."

With that, she stormed out of the jail, slamming the door behind her.

Fendall said, "Lady ought to have her brains counted."

"When you finish counting hers," Bailey said, "count your own. But for now, get up and put your boots on. We're going out to find Axel Gallagher." Fendall Harper knew the territory as well as anyone — might be wise to have him along.

"I said let's get going, Fendall." Bailey prodded him with the tip of his boot. Fendall had dozed off. Bailey got the fire bucket, which was half filled with water."

"Still thirsty, Fendall?" he said.

He poured the water onto Fendall's head. He didn't even stir, just snored.

Bailey thought, *there has to be an easier way to make a living.*

As Bailey and Fendall Harper saddled up, Bailey looked up toward the heavens. Even with the heavy clouds, that damned yellow ball was still in the sky. It was a little bigger today. He pushed away the dark thoughts of what it could inflict on the town — heck, the whole territory.

Doc Cutwater told Bailey the day before, "Some of the folks in town are acting all . . . well, unusual. On Monday, Buck Birdwell tried taking his pants off over his head — his sweetmeats will be swollen for a week. And yesterday, Mose Waddle's wife, Effie, slammed him in the head with a frying pan that was still dirty from breakfast. You know Effie — she's a meek little thing, wouldn't swat a fly. Darn near took his head off."

Now Axel Gallagher never came home. *What next,* Bailey wondered.

He got his answer five minutes later. A massive bolt of lightning momentarily turned night into day, followed by a crack of thunder unlike any Bailey had ever heard, as though the Good Lord had burped after eating Miss Amelia's chili.

The skies opened up — first came the hail, which bounced off their heads, then the torrential rains, which were like a solid sheet of water. The winds kicked up something fierce, close to forty miles an hour, Bailey calculated.

Another bolt of lightning flashed across the landscape, followed by another boomer even louder than before. The horses got skittish. The heavy rain all but turned the dirt trail into a river of mud.

"I can't see through all this muck," Fendall said from behind him. "Not even your horse's rump."

"It still looks the same," Bailey said over the howling winds and rain — which showed no signs of letting up. And the horses were indeed getting skittish. So was, it seemed, Fendall.

"I say we go back, Billy, 'fore we both get drownded," he said. "We couldn't find Axel in this even if the dumb cluck was standing two feet away."

This much was true.

"You're right for the first time in your life," Bailey said. "Let's head back to town."

As they turned their horses around, Fendall said, "I was right one time before

— me 'n' Ben Dillingham was moving a herd down there in Newton County when I said to him, 'Looks like quicksand.' Ol' Ben says, 'Let's take a look-see' and that was the last time I saw him." He added, with a hint of pride, "But I was right."

"Tell that to Ben Dillingham," Bailey said.

To smooth things over — if that was even possible — Bailey invited Agnes Jean and her Aunt Tinky to dine with him at Cantalupo's Italian Spaghetti Palace, the newly opened establishment where a man's belly didn't hurt during the digestive process.

The Cantalupos were Joseph and his wife Josephina, newly arrived Italian immigrants from the Sicilian village of Lercara Friddi. Italian food was something new to Sourwood and in fact, it was the only restaurant of its kind in West Texas. In the courtyard behind the eatery, Josephina grew tomatoes, garlic, oregano, and other spices that gave her marinara sauce a nice kick.

Joseph Cantalupo was a hard-working, honest man but with a temper. He once threw a customer out the door when he asked for ketchup.

"Infamnia!" he said. *"Gavonioni."* Joseph and Josephina were still mastering the intricacies of the American language.

Fendall Harper had once suggested Joseph put up a sign that read "English Broken Here."

Josephina greeted them warmly, sat them at the best table in the house.

"Ah, Marshal Deputy Beeley," she said. "Meese Angus Jean, Meese Tinky, *ciao bella*!"

"*Buona sera,* Miss Josie," Bailey said. *"Tutto bene?"*

"Bene, grazie," Josephina said.

"Who's Benny Grotzi?" Aunt Tinky asked.

"He's speaking Eye-talian to her," Agnes Jean whispered. "It means 'I'm fine, thank you.' "

"How's he know Eye-talian words?" Aunt Tinky asked.

She sniffed the air — the delightful aroma of garlic and oregano wafted from the kitchen. They could hear Joseph singing in Italian.

"What is that I smell?" Aunt Tiny asked. "Reeks like an old slaughterhouse in August."

Agnes Jean kicked her under the table.

"Aunt Tinky meant to say that she's excited about trying your delicious vittles," Agnes Jean said.

"I said nothing of the kind," Aunt Tinky snapped. "I said it smells like —"

"Like heaven," Bailey said. "She said it smells like heaven."

Josephina nodded. *"Si, il paradiso!"*

"If this is what heaven smells like," Aunt Tinky said, "put me on the next stagecoach to hell."

"That's enough, Miss Tinky," Bailey said.

Joseph Cantalupo came out of the kitchen, grinning proudly from ear to ear. He was carrying a massive tureen filled with spaghetti swimming in marinara sauce. Bailey almost started drooling.

"Ah, my *paisano,* Marshal Deputy Beeley," he said, placing the tureen on the table. To Agnes Jean he said, "*Ciao bella,* Meece Jean Agnes!" To Aunt Tinky, he said, *"Sei un rompi cazzoi, signorina Teenky."*

Joseph started dishing out the spaghetti while Josephina filled their glasses with red wine.

"What did he say?" Aunt Tinky wanted to know.

Billy said, "He said you're a pain in the — he said you're painful to look at with all your beauty."

"Is that what he said?" Agnes Jean asked.

"It's close enough," Bailey said, emptying his wine glass and pouring himself another.

"How do you know so many Eye-talian

words?" Aunt Tinky asked.

"Oh, I've picked up some words here and there," Bailey said.

Aunt Tinky glanced down at her plate, piled high with spaghetti. "Looks like a gaggle of bloody nightcrawlers."

Bailey almost choked. Yes, indeed — though neither was on the menu, heartburn and indigestion were going to be for dessert.

It had been little more than a week since the fire in the sky had first appeared but it seemed to be growing in size and each day it was bigger.

Folks in Sourwood were scared silly of the big rock in the sky. Doc Cutwater said to Bailey the next day, "You best call a town meeting, Billy, before out and out panic rips this town to shreds."

Bailey did just that — he sent Fendall out to spread the word. "Town council is having a meeting at 6 PM to address your concerns about the end of the world!"

"I'd have phrased it a little differently," he said to Fendall.

Almost everyone in town showed up; usually, no one gave a hoot about town council meetings — always the same fatheads complaining about the same silly stuff over and over.

This was different.

Bailey and Doc Cutwater stood on the podium, since there was no mayor to chair the meet. Bailey asked Doc Cutwater to address the crowd, as he was considered the smartest man in town.

Folks were rowdy and the meeting threatened to spiral out of control, so Doc grabbed the late mayor's gavel and slammed it down hard to get their attention, missing Bailey's right hand by an inch.

"Everybody shut up!" Doc Cutwater bellowed. Silence fell over the town hall. "As you all have seen, there's a ball of fire in the sky."

"Is it really the end of the world?" asked Mervin Milgrim, the telegrapher. "Are we all doomed to spend eternity burning in hell?"

"It's where you belong, Mervin Milgrim!" This from Aunt Tinky. No surprise there.

"I do not believe this is an act of God," Doc Cutwater said.

"How about an act of Satan?" Aunt Tinky again.

"Simmer down, Tinky," Doc said, and she did. He was the only soul in town she respected. "To be honest, you folks know about as much as we do. But we aim to —"

"It's the end of days, that's what it is!"

said Purvis Peck. There were cries of agreement from the townsfolk.

"Your daddy would've known what to do!" shouted Miss Abigail Wurm, the town gossip.

This brought a chorus of cheers. "I wish he was here!"

"My thoughts exactly!" This from Mavis Grubb, the schoolmarm. "We got hell and damnation staring us right in the face and you don't do nothin'."

"Less than nothin'," Purvis Pike added.

"A gopher'd be a better lawman than you!" Miss Abigail Wurm again. Other voices joined the discussion.

"He's a coward, is what he is."

"Got no more spine than a rattlesnake."

"He ain't got nothin' under his hat but hair."

"He couldn't hit a bull's rump with a handful of banjos."

"He don't give two whoops and a holler 'bout us!"

"He's all cattle and no hat!"

This brought another chorus of cheers. Bailey's ears turned beet red, his face flushed with anger. Then an older man, sitting in the back row, stood. He was dressed in his finest Confederacy uniform, plain double-breasted frock coat — despite the heat — and wearing a flat-crowned rolled brim hat.

He picked up his chair and threw it right through the window of the meeting hall. Glass shattered, sounding like a cannon shot.

It got the folks' attention.

"Close your fat traps and open your dang ears, all of you," the older man said. He looked like someone accustomed to giving orders — and having those orders obeyed.

"Some of you may know me, and for those that don't, I am Brigadier General Noah T. Blunt, 5th Texas Infantry, Retired. And a bigger bunch of lily-livered, weak-kneed sob-sisters I've never seen. Deputy William Bailey is doing *exactly* what his late father would have done."

"And what would that be, Mr. Blunt?" Aunt Tinky asked, her words dripping with venom.

"That's Brigadier General Blunt to you, ma'am."

"We know who you are," Aunt Tinky said.

"Young William's daddy, Braddock Bailey, him and me rode with the Texas Rangers dang near forty years ago. Side by side we fought the Battle of Plum Creek, year of Our Lord eighteen and forty, after the Comanche raided settlements in Linville and Victoria and burned them to the ground, pillagin' and rapin' settlers. Two hundred of us agin' a thousand Apache. I ain't never seen anyone fight like Brad Bailey — with three bullets in him, he still killed half a dozen Comanche by his own gun and woulda killed more iffen them heathens hadn't retreated. He was a man of great courage; in his blood it was. Braddock Bailey was fearless, wasn't afraid of nobody, and always gave more than he got.

"Durin' the War of Northern Aggression, Braddock and me joined up with the Confederacy and killed us our share of bluebelly Yankees."

Purvis Pike opened his mouth to say something. Blunt shot him a look like daggers. Pike wisely kept his mouth shut.

"His daddy fought and bled for Sourwood, a town he loved and dedicated his life to protectin' before the fever took him from us. A braver man I've ever seen, and a more loyal and trusted friend I've ever had or will have again.

"It's been said that an apple doesn't fall far from the tree," Blunt continued. "Well, up there is the apple, Braddock's boy William Thaddeus, who got as much guts and grit as his daddy, and loves Sourwood as much as his daddy did. So if you whinin' fools, who don't know a skunk from a house cat, wanna keep on livin', you'd be wise to do as he says. And if any of you blowflies think you can do a better job, stand up now."

No one did.

Blunt turned and walked out the door, slamming it hard.

"Thank you, Brigadier General," Bailey said.

The crowd started up again. Doc Cutwater tried to get the meeting back on track.

"We have no proof whatsoever that the ball of fire will strike Sourwood," Doc said. "In fact —"

"I ain't hanging around long enough to find out," said Mervin Milgrim. "Come sun-up, me and mine are lightin' out for —"

Agnes Jean, sitting next to her Aunt Tinky, stood and asked, "For where, Mervin? Some of us would like to know."

"Hush, girl!" Aunt Tinky snarled, grabbing Agnes Jean's arm and trying to sit her down.

"Good question," Doc Cutwater said. "Where to, Mervin? I'd say Sourwood isn't the only place that fireball is showing itself."

Mervin Milgrim chimed in again. "Could be, Doc," he said. "But I reckon we got the right to try and see for our ownselves."

More murmurs of agreement. Louder this time.

Bailey said, "We tried sending messages to Austin and Dallas, but the telegraph wires are down, from the storm. We ain't got the means to fix 'em, either."

"More reason to skedaddle, I say," said Edgar "Windy" Leach, a farmer, so named because everything he ate, in his words, gave him the wind.

"Okay," Bailey said. "Let's see a show of hands — those who are fixin' to leave, raise 'em now."

Almost every hand went up. Some folks used both.

"Well fine," Bailey snapped, madder than a wet hen. "Run if you're of a mind to, but don't come slinkin' back with your tails between your legs when this whole thing blows over."

"Ain't nothing blowin' over," said Windy Leach, who made rickety furniture. "Not this time."

After everyone had gone, Doc said to Bailey, "I believe it was William Shakespeare who said 'Lord, what fools these mortals be!' "

" 'All the world's a stage, so let's rob it,' " Fendall added

"Did Shakespeare say that?" Bailey asked.
"Beats me," Fendall said.

Chapter 9

"We shoulda waited at the Buckskin Joe's stage stop back in San Angelo till this storm blew over," Gordie Hochheiser said to the driver, Delmar Futts.

The wind was howling, the rain coming down in buckets, making it difficult to see the road ahead and turning it into a muddy slog.

"In the last fifteen years, I've driven this stage through tornadoes, floods, prairie fires, even a blizzard or two," Futts said over the incessant howling of the wind. "But I ain't never seen nothin' like this."

Hochheiser, who'd been riding shotgun on the Butterworth Stagecoach company for the last few years with Delmar Futts, tried to shake off the uneasy feeling that something was . . . wrong somehow. Nothing he could nail down — maybe it was the raging storm . . . or maybe a tornado was in their future.

Inside the stagecoach, Mrs. Olive Higgins Prouty clutched her husband Eustace's hand as the stage whipped back and forth from the gusting winds. The rain was coming down so heavily it was darn near impossible to see more than a few yards out the window. A bolt of lightning struck a live oak tree and seconds later came the roar of thunder so ear-shattering the entire stagecoach seemed to shake.

"Oh, Eustace!" Mrs. Prouty practically jumped into her husband's lap.

"Unhand me, woman!" Eustace Prouty said, pushing her away. *Twenty years married to this fish-faced, high-strung, needy, always jittery woman,* Prouty thought with a degree of disgust he was finding harder and harder to hide.

To the man sitting opposite him, he said, "One would think the company would have known better than to send us out in this kind of weather. Oh, the Butterworth people will hear of this. I am acquainted with Gunther Stanky, the general manager in San Angelo. Though he's known to be a peckerwood."

"I don't think anyone at Butterworth saw this coming," the man said. He was about forty, well-dressed, with a handlebar moustache and radiated an air of importance.

"And for your information, sir, I am that peckerwood. I don't believe we've been formally introduced. Mr. Gunther Stanky at your service." He pulled something from his vest pocket and handed it to Prouty. "My card."

"Oh, Eustace," Mrs. Prouty gasped. "I've told you to never —"

"Be silent, woman," her husband snapped.

Outside, the storm showed no signs of weakening. If anything, the rain was coming down even heavier now. Hochheiser said, "We best find shelter before the whole territory is underwater."

"Yeah," Futts said. "And that lightning ain't no birthday celebration, neither."

Hochheiser asked, "Is today your birthday?"

"Yes," Futts said. "Forty years old. And I'd like to make it to forty-one. We need to stop and wait this storm out."

Hochheiser was silent for a moment, then said ruefully, "I had no idea . . . I didn't get you a present."

"No worries," Futts said. "I won't get you one when it's your birthday."

Up ahead, a tree had fallen across the trail, blocking it completely. Futts stopped the stagecoach.

"Oh hell," Futts said.

Out of the gloom, Stuffy Grandstaff appeared, armed with a shotgun. He yelled, "Stand and deliver!"

"Can I ask a dumb question?" Hochheiser asked.

"No one does it better," Futts said.

"Are we being robbed?"

"Kinda looks that way."

Stuffy barked, "Throw down your rifles, dogfaces, and climb on down here." He sneezed twice.

Hochheiser grumbled, "Who's a dogface?" but he dutifully tossed his rifle out. Futts did as well, but pushed the butt of his pistol down under his pants and out of sight. The two men jumped down, hands in the air. Stuffy kicked their rifles away and gave a whistle. Out of the fog came Dex McGoon, Mossy Grandstaff, and a new addition to the welcoming party, Sneed Hearn, who'd just joined the McGoon Gang not long after the bank robbery. McGoon spotted him in a crummy cantina, where someone commented, "As a deadly shot, no one can touch him. As a human being, no one *wants* to touch him."

Hearn was a particularly vicious outlaw who'd killed, by his own estimate, fifteen men and a couple of women, too. He didn't say much — his ferocious countenance, adorned with a jagged scar down his left cheek, an eyepatch on his right orb, and one ear that looked like it had been chewed off, spoke for itself.

McGoon said to Stuffy, "I don't suppose you asked these gentlemen for the cashbox?"

"The what?" Stuffy asked.

McGoon said to Mossy Grandstaff, "Get the bleeding cashbox." To Stuffy, he said, "Halfwit."

While Grandstaff rooted around for the cashbox, usually kept under the driver's seat, he came up empty.

"Ain't none," Grandstaff said.

"If was off-loaded back in Weasel Creek," Futts said.

McGoon smiled indulgently and said, "Now, ain't that a shame." He flung open the stagecoach door and said to the passengers, waving the barrel of his rifle at them, "Okay, folks, everybody out."

They did as they were told. Mrs. Prouty got out first. Sneed Hearn reached out to help her down. She gasped, getting a good look at that battered face. "Don't touch me! Leave me be, you heathen," she said. Her husband Eustace and Mr. Stanky followed.

"Oh, don't be worryin' about old Sneed here," McGoon said. "He's a great lover of humanity. It's people he hates."

McGoon reached in and lifted the seat formerly occupied by Mr. Stanky. Underneath, as McGoon had suspected, was the cashbox. The lock was as big and thick as his fist. He hefted it out and swung it into the mud. McGoon jumped out of the stage and fired, blowing the lock into pieces.

McGoon turned to Futts. "You do know it's a sin to tell a lie," he said, and shot Futts in the throat. Futts grabbed his throat as blood spurted out in a heavy stream between his fingers. He staggered a few times then went face-down into the mud.

Mrs. Prouty started screaming — likewise her husband. Mr. Stanky was too stunned to react at all.

"Del!" Hochheiser shouted at McGoon. "You lowdown scum, you filthy pigs, you —"

"Aw, shut your big yap," McGoon said, and shot Hochheiser right in the heart, dropping him where he stood.

Mrs. Prouty continued bellowing, getting on McGoon's nerves. He nodded at Sneed Hearn, who nodded back and shot Mrs. Prouty straight into her gut, jerking her backwards against the stagecoach. She slumped to the ground, her lifeless eyes still wide in shock. Hearn turned the rifle on Eustace Prouty and plugged him as well, taking off a good portion of his face.

Hearn turned the rifle on Mr. Stanky, who said, "I don't suppose you'd like to discuss this . . ."

"Ain't nothing to discuss," McGoon said. "Mr. Hearn, please do the honors."

Sneed Hearn blasted Stanky, lifting the man right off his feet. Stanky went to his reward, however unwillingly.

"Think he's dead?" Stuffy asked.

"If not, his stagecraft is superb," McGoon replied. He kicked over the cashbox. In it was eighteen dollars in cash, some useless bonds, and silver coins.

"Looks like this just ain't our day, Dex," Stuffy commented.

CHAPTER 10

The massive, blazing space rock was clearly getting larger with each passing day, bigger to the naked eye than the sun and the moon. The storms, caused by the unusual weather, knocked out the telegraph wires (which were never that reliable anyway), so Sourwood was cut off from the rest of the world.

In town, Deputy Sheriff William Bailey was having a very bad day. Or year, as events in Sourwood were spiraling; the townsfolk were doing their best to cope with what seemed to be the destruction of all life on Earth. Lomax Milligan, the barber, now had three other men helping him dig his "shelter." Other folks in town commandeered Milligan's idea and were also digging their own holes. All over town what looked like giant anthills were popping up as people sought salvation underground.

The prairie was silent — no howling of

wolves, no trilling of birds, no sign of any armadillos, and even the field mice and rattlesnakes were nowhere to be seen.

Following the storms that half-flooded the territory, a sizzling heat wave engulfed the region, prompting Fendall Harper to comment, "This is Death Valley kinda hot." Sourwood's part of Texas was no stranger to brutal strength-sapping heat, but the temps had risen to 104 degrees and stayed that way even at night with no relief in sight.

Between the heat and the impending doom, residents of Sourwood were half-crazed with fear. Fights were breaking out, along with what sounded like gunfire. Husbands and wives are at each other's throats — more than usual.

Earlier that morning, Bailey, with Fendall Harper's help, had to break some sweaty heads over to the Saddle Sore Saloon, where half a dozen customers got into a vicious brawl over the very last bottle of rotgut whiskey. Since the emergence of Mr. Blinky, whiskey shipments came to a grinding halt. No beer, either. Sourwood's less than honest denizens were stealing anything that wasn't nailed down at some of the town's businesses.

Bailey already surmised that some folks to pack up and leave but they seemed resigned to their fiery fate, mournfully saying, "What's the use?" The widow Arabella Webley, however, who was not content with this grim attitude, walked into Sturdley's Mercantile, grabbed a new broom, and proceeded to walk out again, with nary a worry. When Mr. Sturdley said, "That broom is fifty cents, Miss Arabella."

She responded, "Doomsday or no doomsday, ain't nobody ever gonna say I left behind a dirty home."

At noon, Bailey was trying to take a break between the saloon brawls, husbands beating their wives — sometimes wives beating husbands — and their kids running wild and setting fires.

He was trying to decide how to squelch Sourwood's spiraling unrest. Maybe the people were right; what *was* the use?

There was a saying about death and taxes being the two major certainties, but there was a third one. At noon sharp Miss Amelia came into the sheriff's office carrying Bailey's lunch on a napkin-covered tray. She never missed one of Bailey's meals.

She set the tray on Bailey's desk, and said, "Enjoy."

Bailey pulled the napkin away. On the plate was a slab of rotten, uncooked beef. The foul aroma hit his nostrils and his eyes actually crossed. Upon closer inspection, Bailey noticed an army of grubs crawling on top of it. His stomach did a flip-flop.

"What in the name of the Lord is this, Miss Amelia?"

She said, "Lunch?"

"This meat is rotten!" Bailey said.

"Well, look who just caught on," Miss Amelia said.

"If this is a joke, Miss Amelia?" Bailey said, "I ain't laughing. How can you serve me this?"

"It wasn't me," she said. "You may want to discuss it with Wolfie Dunderbeck. This is what he delivered this morning."

"Wolfie Dunderbeck the butcher?" Bailey asked.

"He's the only one we got, Billy."

"Let's go talk to him," Bailey said. He felt deep worry gnawing at his insides.

Wolfgang Dunderbeck — everyone called him Wolfie — had emigrated from a town in Germany called Schvitzbergen not long after the end of the War of Northern Aggression.

Many Germans had settled into this part of Texas. A butcher by trade, Dunderbeck very much looked the part. He was six-foot three, a solid wall of muscle. His massive forearms were bigger than the branches of a live oak tree.

Dunderbeck had a small shop a few hundred feet from the mercantile. He'd built his own smokehouse, where he salted the fresh beef to draw out moisture and then hung it to dry, creating a ten-foot line of jerky.

Dunderbeck was proud that he could smoke virtually anything — squirrels, pigeons, rabbits, wild ducks, deer, and even an occasional wild boar.

As Miss Amelia and Bailey entered Dunderbeck's little shop, the foul aroma of rotting beef and chickens almost knocked them over. The strips of beef jerky were covered in flies. Dunderbeck was wearing an apron splattered with blood and was in the process of slamming a huge butcher knife into a smelly chicken.

Miss Amelia placed the rotten meat on the counter and said, "You want to tell me what this is, Mr. Dunderbeck?"

He didn't look up from his work. He said, "Is beef."

"No," Miss Amelia said. "You mean it *used* to be beef. Now it's a hotel for bugs."

"Meat good," Dunderbeck maintained, though he didn't look like he believed it. He continued chopping away. Bailey chose to ignore the giant rat skittering across the floor with a slab of beef jerky in its mouth.

"Meat not good, Wolfie," Bailey said. "Meat make people sick."

"Put meat over fire, kill bugs. Then meat fine."

"You don't understand, Wolfie," Bailey said. "Selling meat you know is bad is against the law. I could put you in jail!'

Dunderbeck slammed the meat cleaver down on the counter and said, looking resigned, "Heat too hot for root cellar — meat from chicken, pig, cow all go bad."

Bailey and Miss Amelia didn't need convincing. The rancid aroma of rotting meat wafted up from the fruit cellar. Miss Amelia put a hanky over her nose and mouth. Dunderbeck went back to chopping.

"Wolfie," Bailey said, "folks who eat that steak could die of food poisoning."

Dunderbeck looked up and pointed to the heavens.

He said, "Vat difference it make now?"

Chapter 11

Agnes Jean was driving Sturdley's buckboard wagon, filled with the meager supplies, down Main Street when she spotted Bailey sitting outside the jailhouse, looking lost and utterly dejected. There were several townsfolk in the jail: Colton Sweeney, for beating the stuffing out of Wally Wallace; Wally Wallace for pummeling Colton Sweeney back and throwing him through the glass picture window of the cobbler shop. The fight stemmed from the lack of whiskey in town. Nooner had shut down the Saddle Sore — a man couldn't even get a flat beer.

At high noon, things were unusually quiet in Sourwood. For the moment, anyway. At dusk is when things got hopping — fistfights, sounds of gunshots, some looting, and Bailey's new favorite, people standing in the street screaming at the big yellow ball in the sky as if that would do any good. Not that he blamed them — he wanted to scream at it himself.

Agnes Jean stopped the buckboard. Even in these seriously trying times, she looked fresh and full of life. Bailey could feel himself becoming aroused. He looked down and murmured, “Your timing really stinks, old friend.”

Agnes Jean asked Bailey, “Everything okay there, Billy? You look like someone ate your puppy.”

That would make it muttloaf Bailey thought crazily, and wondered if he, too, was going soft in the head. A glance up at the sky showed the unwanted arrival of God’s wrath getting closer still.

He said, “Oh, sure, all is well. The world is ending in a blazing ball of fire, Sourwood is about to be wiped off the face of the earth, and if that ain’t bad enough, the Saddle Sore is out of whiskey.”

“Ah, the crosses we bear,” Agnes Jean said. “Wanna go for a little jaunt?

“Why not?” Bailey said. He hopped onto the buckboard.

The wagon was carrying a few wooden boxes of canned food and cleaning stuff like brushes and soap.

He said, “Forgot today is your weekly visit.” He wiped sweat off his forehead —

the heat was brutal still, even by Texas standards. He hopped up onto the seat of the buckboard and took the reins from Agnes Jean.

Bailey knew the way blindfolded. He jerked the wagon to a halt in front of a tar-paper shack nestled under a sprawling sycamore tree. The shack had seen better days, but then so did the lady who lived there.

On what was left of the front porch — half of it had sunk into the ground — sat an impossibly old woman with white hair that flowed down to her tiny waist. She couldn't have stood more than four-foot-five or weighed in at ninety pounds. Even ten feet away, it was easy to see she had no teeth.

Esmerelda decided she'd had enough of the Comanche life and one day walked away from the reservation. No one attempted to stop her — and she settled in what was now the town of Sourwood. Married a prospector, name of Aaron Chance, and they built the crumbling shack she had called home ever since. She kept the name Esmerelda — it was the only name she knew.

Ordinarily, Esmerelda would have been seen as yet one more oddball in Sourwood and ignored, except for one thing: Miss Esmerelda *saw* things. Not events that had already occurred, but events that had yet to happen. When Travis and Daisy Cutter's four-year-old son, Tyler, went missing, Miss Marfi told Marshal Bailey — Bill's late father — that the boy had been looking for nightcrawlers and wandered off. That was pretty much what everyone surmised but Miss Esmerelda drew a crude map of the tiny bit of swamp where the nightcrawlers existed in abundance. And a part of the forest few knew even existed.

That's where they found Tyler, no worse for the wear. And how Esmerelda knew where Tyler had gotten to became the stuff of legend. Even more curious was that she had gone blind forty years earlier.

Agnes Jean climbed off the wagon and called out, louder than necessary but most folks seem to think yelling compensated for Esmerelda's blindness, "We're here with supplies, Miss Esmerelda." Bailey hopped down and started unloading baskets of essentials — corn, flower, sugar, salt, honey, canned peaches, whichever vegetables she could scrape up. This shipment to Esmerelda's was maybe a quarter of what it was before the Good Lord started playing with fireballs in the heavens. Bailey whistled as he unloaded the supplies.

Miss Esmerelda banged her walking stick

on the porch and a chubby young Mexican woman came out of the shack. Her name was Lupita and she was the only person in the world Miss Esmerelda would communicate with.

Miss Esmerelda whispered something in Lupita's ear. Lupita nodded and said to Agnes Jean, "Senora Esmerelda say to tell you she blind, not deef."

Miss Esmerelda whispered something else in Lupita's ear.

Lupita said, "Senora Esmerelda want to know if man with you is William Bailey."

"Yes . . . but how did she know that?" Agnes Jean said a little nervously.

Another whisper in Lupita's ear. Lupita said, "Miss Esmerelda say Senor Bailey whistle just like his daddy did."

"I gucss I do," Bailey said, realizing he'd never really been aware that he whistled at all, much less like his father had

Bailey was carrying crates and baskets into Miss Esmerclda's shack. Inside was a bed, a dresser, a table, a stove, a few rickety chairs, a chest of drawers, and that was about it. Miss Esmerelda clearly led a very spartan existence.

Bailey started unpacking the boxes and putting cans of peaches on the bottom shelves. Outside, he heard Lupita holler,

"Senora Esmerelda say peaches go on top shelf."

That chore done, Bailey came out and motioned for Agnes Jean to get back aboard the wagon to return to town.

"Can Miss Esmerelda really predict what the future holds?" Bailey asked Lupita, his curiosity getting the better of him.

Lupita nodded, saying, "*Si,* senora Esmerelda know what happen before it happen. Last *Sabato* she say it going to rain, and on *Domingo* it did."

"That's hardly being able —" Bailey started to say.

Miss Esmerelda whispered something into Lupita's ear. "Senora Esmerelda also say everyone going to be perishing very soon."

Bailey and Agnes Jean froze. "She said what?" Agnes Jean asked.

"Is big ball of fire in sky is why *personas* . . ." She paused and Miss Esmerelda whispered something. Lupita continued, "Has *personas* little green *manzanas.*"

"Little green what?" Bailey asked.

"Manzanas," Lupita said, a little irritably. "What's matter con you, you no speak Ingles?"

"When you speak it, I'll understand it," Bailey muttered.

"Senora Esmerelda say —"

"Does Senora Esmerelda ever talk to anyone but you?" Bailey asked.

"She used to talk to herself," Lupita said, "but she stop when say she get too many stupid answers."

"If Miss Esmerelda is blind, how does she know about the big fire in the sky?" Agnes Jean asked.

"Miss Esmerelda always know what happen before it happen," Lupita said. "I no say a word but Miss Esmerelda, she feel it. She say the Almighty making us atone for our sins by burning up us."

Bailey still wasn't buying it, though his hopes that this crisis would end soon were fading. "And when will this ball of fire destroy us?" he asked.

"When it damn well pleases, you peckerwoods!" Miss Esmerelda shouted. "The heat gets hotter with each passing day. Might be a week, maybe two, but the Lawd has plans for us and ain't no one going to like 'em."

"I thought you said she didn't speak to anyone," Bailey said.

"Only when she . . . how you say . . . peesed off."

Miss Esmerelda lifted herself out of the rocker and handed Lupita a little burlap bundle she had on her lap and motioned for her to give it to Agnes Jean.

Lupita said, "Senora Esmerelda say you give to Senor Sturdley at mercantile to pay for these things."

Agnes Jean took it — felt a little heavy for cash money. She unwrapped the soiled handkerchief. Inside was a yellow rock that weighed maybe five ounces. It glinted in the sunlight.

"She paying with rocks now?" Bailey asked.

"If this is what I think it is, it's no ordinary rock," Agnes Jean said. "I do believe it's . . . gold."

Bailey looked at the rock again. He said to Lupita, "Where did you get this?"

Lupita said, "Senor Esmerelda give it to me to give it to you to give it to Senor Sturdley."

"What is it?" Bailey asked.

"Oro," she said. "Gold. Senora Esmerelda's get from her husband. He bring her home mucho oro. Then he die."

"Well then, where is it?" Bailey asked.

Lupita shook her head. "Senora Esmerelda only one who know where *oro* is buried and she not even tell me."

Bailey said to Agnes Jean, "Let's have a little jaw-boning with your boss, Mr. Sturdley."

■ ■ ■ ■

"Ms. Esmerelda has never paid me with cash money," Chester Sturdley said as he wrapped a catfish — one that didn't smell too fresh. Even the catfish in nearby Horseshoe Lake were swimming deeper and deeper.

He looked at the nugget Agnes Jean had given him. He went into the back room and came back holding an old cigar box. Inside were at least three dozen nuggets.

"Old Miss Esmerelda hasn't seen cash money since James Madison was in the White House," Sturdley said. "This is what she uses for bartering."

"Is it real actual gold?" Agnes Jean asked.

"No idea," Sturdley said. "But I couldn't let the old gal starve, could I?"

"Oh, it's real gold, and no mistake," Doc Cutwater said, standing in the mercantile doorway, as if the breeze had plopped him down. He pulled a nugget from his pocket. "Miss Esmerelda gave me this five years ago after I took care of her chilblain. She's the only one who knows where it's buried and she ain't talking."

"Where the heck did she get all that gold?" Bailey wanted to know.

"She was married to a prospector, name of Otis Hinkley, who struck it big at Sutter's Mill back in '49," Sturdley said.

"Hinkley's heart gave out not long after he returned to Sourwood and buried his newfound riches," Doc Cutwater said.

"Then why hasn't she turned all that gold into cash money?" Agnes Jean asked. "And built a big house instead of that shack she lives in now?"

Doc Cutwater said, "I suspect that if she ever spoke publicly about the gold, she'd have been overrun with all the jaspers in the territory trying to find it. And that shack has been her home for darn near fifty years. You couldn't blast her out of that hovel with a ton of dynamite."

"And if she took it to the bank," Sturdley said, "word would spread like wildfire."

"Mr. Sturdley and I made a solemn promise to each other — when was that, Chester?" Doc Cutwater asked.

"Right after the war ended," Sturdley said. "We promised not to mention the gold, not even to each other. And we never have."

Doc said, "I've known her since I started my practice here, more years ago than I care to remember, and after all this time I think I can safely say this: nobody, and I mean nobody, knows what Miss Esmerelda will do or why."

"All this gold," Sturdley said wistfully, holding a few nuggets, "would fetch me a king's ransom. And now there ain't no time left to spend it."

"Could things get any worse?" Agnes Jean said.

"Well yes, Miss Aggie, they could," Sturdley said. "Ain't got much of anything left to sell, so I got to let you go." He handed her a gold nugget. "This'll cover what I owe you."

"Thank you, Mr. Sturdley," Agnes Jean said, "but you might as well keep it. As the saying goes, 'you can't take it with you.' "

"Take what?" Sturdley asked.

Chapter 12

Bailey really could have used a beer — even Tubby Nooner's watered down swill — but there wasn't a beer bubble to be found in Sourwood. Anyway, Nooner had shuttered the Saddle Sore — no beer, no booze, no business. Even his small supply of sarsaparilla was gone.

Bailey sat dejectedly at his battered wooden desk. Folks in Sourwood — those that hadn't skedaddled — were starting to go loco. The impending doom affected people differently but as the ball of fire approached a little more each day, their cheese slid off their crackers just a little bit more.

Earlier that day, Bailey had seen Wolfie Dunderbeck chasing some kids with a meat cleaver, but fortunately, the kids were faster. Mrs. Alma Whitworth, the schoolmarm, strolled casually down Main Street as naked as a jaybird with nothing but a parasol.

Fendall Harper was snoring away on one

of the bunks in the jail cell. He'd been sober four days now and it didn't agree with him.

He mumbled in his sleep, "Aw now, Honey Mae, I cain't take you for another roll in the hay . . . gotta drive them cattle to . . . now Honey Mae, don't be doing that . . ."

Bailey had no idea who Honey Mae was — someone from Fendall's wicked past no doubt. Probably a working gal from the stockyards in Fort Worth. Fendall had never taken a wife — his reputation was such that no lady with a brain in her noggin would put up with his carousing and boozing. Word was, he single-handedly kept Honey Mae Gribble's Happy Times cathouse in business. He also kept Honey Mae in business.

Fendall suddenly awakened with a snort, a cough, and another snort.

"Good morning," Bailey said. "Who's Honey Mae?"

Fendall blew his nose into a filthy rag. He said, "Was I jawboning in my sleep again?"

Bailey nodded. "Sounded like you were having fun."

"Honey Mae . . . been years," Fendall remembered with a smile. "That gal could please a man in ways even Mother Nature never dreamed of."

"Would she please you if she was here now?"

"Not hardly," Fendall said. "Wouldn't be much use no how. Hell, at my age, it'd take me all night to do what I used to do all night."

"Right," Bailey said, holstering up for his daily rounds. "Just don't do it here, if you know what I mean."

Without waiting for a response, Bailey wandered outside. The town was silent. The comet seemed even closer today.

He heard the buckboard wagon before he saw it lumbering sluggishly down Main Street.

Driving the buckboard was farmer Harry Hoskins and his wife, Myrtle. The buckboard was loaded down with virtually everything the Hoskins clan owned — goose-down mattresses, a kitchen table, chairs, a chest of drawers, clothes, pillows, blankets, the whole deal. Not to mention Hoskins' ten-year-old twin daughters, Daisy and Maisie. Bailey gave them a smile. They giggled as only little girls can.

"Going somewhere, Harry?" Bailey asked. He took off hat and bowed slightly for Harry's wife. "Miz Hoskins," he greeted.

"Yeah, we're going somewhere," Hoskins said.

"And where would that be?" Bailey asked.

"Anywhere that ain't here," Hoskins said. "Thinkin' about El Paso, maybe Denver. Got a brother there."

"Might not be any better in Denver or even in California," Bailey said. "Maybe the whole world is in for a beating."

"Hogwash," Hoskins said. "And don't go palavering about divine retribution and the wrath of the Lord and end of days like the rest of the Bible thumpers in Sourwood. I don't know what that thing in the sky is but it's fixin' to land right in our laps."

"You don't know that," Bailey said. "I hear-tell it may just pass right over and hit somewhere else — El Paso maybe, or Denver."

"Have it your own way, Billy," Hoskins said. "Maybe you're right and maybe you ain't, but we're leaving." He snapped the reins and the two listless horses moved. Hoskins looked over his shoulder and said, "And you should, too, Billy. Ain't no shame in runnin', not if it means saving your own hide."

Bailey had thought about it, grabbing Agnes Jean — and her Aunt Tinky regrettably — and high-tailing it out of town but deep down he knew he couldn't. Sourwood was home, had been all his days, and when his time came, he would be dying in Sourwood. Just earlier then he'd planned.

"Godspeed, Hoskins," he shouted back.

The door to Lomax Milligan's barber shop was open. Bailey ventured over.

Inside, Milligan was dozing in his barber chair, still clutching his shovel. Bailey had to admit Milligan had dug himself an impressive hole — eight feet deep and four feet wide.

"Wake up, Lomax," Bailey said.

Milligan opened his eyes and shook his head to clear it. He said, "Is it here?"

"Is *what* here?"

"You know what," Milligan snapped. "That big bundle of death and destruction bearing down on us."

"No, not yet," Bailey said. "That is, if it bears down on us at all."

Bailey wasn't completely sure, but Lomax Milligan looked a trifle disappointed. He said, "But it's still coming closer, isn't it?"

"Yes," Bailey admitted. No point in sugarcoating it.

He picked a rock up off the floor — the piles of dirt took up about 90% of his barber shop and reached almost to the ceiling. He tossed it into the hole and it made a splashing sound when it landed.

"There's water at the bottom?" he asked.

"Hit an underground spring or something," Milligan said. "So I reckon the hole isn't as deep as I planned but I'll have to make due."

"Where are all your helpers?"

"They quit," Milligan said. "Gutless wretches. Abel Beaver was first. Said we'd never all fit down there, so he departed."

"Did he now?" Bailey asked.

"Yup," Milligan said angrily.

He wiped the sweat off his face. He said, "The heat is getting hotter."

This was certainly true enough.

"Henry Snavely went next." Milligan wiped his forehead again. "Said he was tired of worms crawling up his pants. Probably the most fun the old goat's had in years."

Bailey let that one slide. He said, "Guess I'll see you around then, Lomax."

"Not if I can help it," Milligan said.

The door to the jailhouse flew open. In ran Beauregard Starkwell, younger son of rancher Jedadiah Starkwell. Beau, all of sixteen, was wild-eyed and frantic, looking like he was about to jump out of his own skin.

"You gotta come with me, Marshal," Beau said, trying to catch his breath. "You gotta come now! Pa says —"

"If it's a matter of life or death," Fendall said, "looks like death got hisself the upper hand."

"What's so urgent, Beau? You come running in here like your ass was on fire," Bailey said.

"Poor choice of words there, Billy," Fendall said. "Given the situation."

Beau exclaimed, "Pa says he knows what's happening and why, what that fire in the sky is all about."

"He ain't bringin' the Almighty into this, is he?" Bailey asked wearily. "I get a bellyful of that from damn near everyone in town."

"Jed Starkwell ain't no Jesus jumper," Fendall said. "Got book learning in spades and has schoolin' all the way to the sixth grade."

"Pa says that is has somethin' to do with the moon," Beau said. "And the stars and all the dark space beyond. I didn't quite catch on to what he was sayin', but my big brother Virgil did. Pa told him to go and fetch Doc Cutwater and bring him to the Bar S. Told me to bring you, too. Says you and Doc are the only souls in town with half a brain, so y'all will unnerstand."

Fendall snorted. "Half a brain, Billy," he said. "Old Jed is feelin' generous today."

Bailey said, "Fetch the horses and let's

saddle up. If Jed Starkwell thinks he can save us from perdition, maybe we ought to hear him out."

Chapter 13

At dusk, the torrential rains returned but they didn't make things any cooler. Despite the grey/black storm clouds, the ball of fire in the sky poked through — where neither the sun nor the moon could. And it was getting bigger still.

At the café, Miss Amelia was reduced to brewing very weak coffee — she'd been using the same grounds for three days.

She was cooking up a pot of mush with what little she had left — old soup bones, cornmeal, baking powder, her last helping of pinto beans, a limp green pepper, mushy apples, and a pound of salt to kill the taste she knew would not be pleasing to her customers. Before he skedaddled, her cook Ninni had tried baking a load of sawdust bread — an ounce of flour, a little shortening, and actual sawdust, which was the only thing plentiful in Sourwood. Some very hungry folks even tried a piece.

"Kept me in the outhouse for two days," said Hiram Barlow, though everyone called him Short Stack due to his almost fanatical love of griddlecakes.

Miss Amelia was getting ready to shut down for the might . . . or shut down forever if supplies couldn't get through. There were a few regulars who sipped her weak coffee and found it impossible to think about anything other than the fire in the sky and impending doom.

The café door opened and in stepped a tall man dressed in black from head to toe. Rainwater dripped off his black bowler. He was smiling, but there was no mirth in it. He took off his hat and bowed slightly.

"Gettin' ready to close up, mister," Miss Amelia told him. "And even if we weren't, ain't got enough grub to fill a hen's tooth."

"I didn't know hens had teeth," Short Stack said.

"It's not sustenance I'm seeking," the stranger said. "I merely need a place to rest my weary old bones."

"Hotel burned to the ground five years ago," Miss Amelia said. All eyes were on the stranger now. "There's Liddiflower Gribble's boarding house down the street but Liddi don't rent rooms to folks she don't know or ain't been referred by those she trusts."

"Well, that does not bode well for my weary bones, does it?" the stranger asks.

"Shoot, man," Short Stack said. He was grumpy. Hadn't enjoyed griddlecakes in five days. "Ever' other house in town is empty. Take your pick."

"And why are so many homes empty?" the stranger asked.

"Unless y'all are blind in both eyes," Miss Amelia said, "maybe you ain't seen what the Good Lord's got waiting for us upstairs. Don't know how much time we got left, but I wouldn't spend it sleepin'."

"Perhaps I should seek lodging elsewhere," the stranger said.

"Good luck," Short Stack said. "It's like this all over creation."

"You got a name, mister?" Miss Amelia asked. She was accustomed to all kinds of oddballs dropping into her café but this one was different. And not necessarily in a good way.

"Goodrich," the stranger said. "Thornton Goodrich. The *Reverend* Thornton Goodrich."

"I know all of the circuit riders who preach in the territory," Miss Amelia said. "Ain't seen you around before."

Goodrich's smile widened a bit. *I can't wait to dismember this little biddy,* he thought.

"I was only ordained a month ago at the Methodist Episcopal Church in Baltimore, Maryland," Goodrich said.

"I been to Baltimore one time," Short Stack said. "Smelled like fish."

"This is my first journey as a man of the Lord," Goodrich said. "I heard about the tragic and untimely passing of Reverend Broadhurst. It is my sworn duty to offer hope, salvation, and redemption to the good people who have none."

"Then I'd venture to say, Reverend, you got your work cut out for you," Miss Amelia said. "The closer that fire in the sky gets, the less people are praying."

"Then all the more reason why they should keep on praying, only harder," Goodrich said. "As the Good Book says, 'Do not seal up the words of the prophecy, for the time is near!' Revelation, Chapter 22, Versc 11."

Miss Amelia said, " 'But immediately after the tribulation of those days the sun will be darkened, and the moon will not give its light, and the stars will fall from the sky, and the powers of the heavens will be shaken.' Matthew, Chapter 24, Verse 29. In other words, Reverend Goodrich, I'd say you're a dollar late and a day short."

"I think it's the other way around, Miss Amelia," Short Stack said. "It's 'A short day and a dollar late.' "

"Heck, take any house you want," Miss Amelia said. "Lot of folks skedaddled without even taking their furniture." She knew instinctively though that events with this Reverend Thornton Goodrich were not going to end well. But then, nothing was going to end well. And he was right about one thing — a little prayer wouldn't hurt anyone.

"Thank you kindly, Miss . . . ?"

"Miss Amelia," she said. "Hope you brought your own vittles, Reverend, cause food's gotten scarce in Sourwood since that ball of fire showed up."

"Weren't all that good before the ball of fire, neither," Short Stack commented.

CHAPTER 14

"It's called a comet," Jedadiah Starkwell said, as if everyone should've known that. "That seems to be what we're dealing with."

"A what?" Fendall asked.

"A comet," Starkwell said. "A big hunk of rock that's been flying around the heavens for millions of years."

"Picked one hell of a time to drop by," Bailey said.

"How do you know this, Jedadiah?" Doc Cutwater asked.

They were all assembled in the living room of the Starkwell homestead, the Bar S — Bailey, Fendall, Doc Cutwater, and Starkwell's two sons, Beau and Virgil — not the sharpest tools in the shed perhaps, but they were hardworking and kept the Bar S going. They fearlessly went after cattle thieves and the assorted lowlife trouble-making scoundrels who made the grave mistake of stealing, or trying to steal, from the Starkwells.

Jedadiah was sixty-six, with a graying muttonchop beard and piercing blue eyes that looked right through to your soul. He was also in a wheelchair, shot in the spine five years earlier by a notorious cattle rustler named Lyle Bonesaw. It was the last shot Bonesaw got off before he was ventilated six ways from Sunday by Starkwell's cowboys.

"Virgil," Starkwell said, pointing to the bookshelf. "Fetch me that big black book, last one on the right, top shelf."

Virgil did as requested, handing his father the dusty volume, which made a crackly sound when Jed opened it. The book was titled *A Brief History of Our World.*

"Been on that shelf close to forty years and I never opened it till today," Starkwell said.

"Pa's a slow reader," Virgil commented.

"Pa reads a lot," Beau said. "Began reading *The Three Musketeers* thirty years ago and he's already up to chapter two," Beau said.

"Pa sez having books in your home make people think you're smart," Virgil added.

"Button your lips, both of you," Starkwell said. "This here picture was drawn by some feller in 1577 named Copernicus. He studied on things like this."

"Copernicus his first name or last name?" Fendall asked.

"I don't rightly know," Starkwell said.

"Gotta be one or t'other," Fendall said.

"Maybe it's both," Bailey said. "Now pipe down, Fendall."

"There have been others, too," Starkwell said. "The — the book says such, but no record of any of 'em punching a whole in the sky and crashing into this world."

Bailey felt a brief glimmer of hope.

They all gathered around Starkwell's wheelchair to look at the drawing. It showed a big orange/red ball with a tail of fire hurtling through space. It looked huge. It looked scary. And it looked deadly.

"Holy Mother of God," Fendall said. "Looks just like ours!"

"It does at that," Doc Cutwater said. He asked Starkwell, "Did this Copernicus say when ours will strike?"

"That's just it," Starkwell said. "He didn't. I suspect we won't know for sure till the damn thing lands on our front porch."

"Well, ain't that a kick in the head," Fendall said. "Starve to death or end up a big mess of fried chicken gizzards."

"Maybe this Mr. Copernicus has a friend who knows," Beau suggested.

"Unless that friend is four hundred years

old," Doc Cutwater said, "I wouldn't put much stock in that."

"Well, that clinches it," Bailey said, visibly irritated. "I don't give a tinker's cuss if it hits tomorrow or twenty years from now, my job is to protect the people of Sourwood and I aim to do just that, come hell or high water."

"We've no doubt of that, Billy," Doc Cutwater said. "Your heart's always been in the right place, just like your father. But just how do you plan on protecting us?"

"I'm gonna face down that comet and give it the dirtiest look it ever got," he said.

"Why don't I feel better?" Fendall wanted to know.

Chapter 15

It was dusk when the McGoon Gang — now reduced to Dex, Mossy Grandstaff, Sneed Hearn, and Stuffy Grandstaff — rode into Sourwood. McGoon had them enter town an hour apart to avoid suspicion, and meet at the saloon.

He said to Snuffy, "Try not to kill anyone."

Snuffy looked disappointed. He said, "Why not?"

McGoon needn't have worried though — the streets were pretty much deserted. A few people scurried here and about but for a Friday evening, things should have been much livelier. Most of the businesses were shuttered — including the saloon,

"Kinda dead in the water hereabouts, ain't it?" Mossy said.

"I seen more action in a San Angelo boneyard," Stuffy said.

"It's that ball of fire in the sky," McGoon said. "Got 'em scared spitless."

"They ain't the only ones," Mossy murmured.

"That ball of fire don't mean squat," McGoon said. "I have it on very good authority it won't come nowhere near close to us."

"On whose authority?" Mossy asked.

"Mine," McGoon said. "Now let's go grab us a drink."

They walked ten feet apart to the Saddle Sore Saloon. McGoon pushed open the batwing doors. The place smelled of rotgut whiskey, sweat, and old tobacco; the aroma of body odor was overpowering.

The Saddle Sore was also empty except for one man in the back, who was throwing darts at the wall. Someone had stolen the target.

Tubby didn't turn around. He said, "You boys here to rob me? Is it money you want?"

McGoon said, "What we want is a bottle of whiskey and four glasses. Clean glasses if possible."

"Can give you the glasses," Tubby said, "but not the whiskey. In case you ain't noticed, there ain't a drop to be had anywhere in the territory. Sorry, gentlemen."

"Beer?" Mossy asked hopefully.

"Not even sodee pop," Tubby said.

"What do folks here do for entertainment?" McGoon asked.

"When they ain't minding their own business, mostly they worry about the end of creation," Tubby said. "You must've seen that big thing in the sky. Kinda hard to miss."

"Oh, we've indeed seen it," McGoon said. "But it ain't the end of the world like you people think."

"It ain't what we think," Tubby said. "It's what the Almighty thinks — and He's got plans for us all."

"Then why has the Almighty waited thousands of years to drop the big rock on y'all?" McGoon asked.

Tubby turned and faced them. The one who did most of the talking looked slightly familiar to him. Tubby couldn't recall where or when but he was sure he'd seen the man somewhere. He suddenly got a nagging feeling in his gut.

"Anything else I can do for you boys?"

Snuffy stepped closer to Tubby and said, snarling, "Yeah, blanket-head. You can give us whiskey like my friend asked for."

He pressed the tip of his Barlow knife under Tubby's chins.

Tubby said, "Mister when I . . . when I . . ."

Snuffy turned his head abruptly, as if having been slapped. Between the foul air and the sawdust on the floor, Stuffy loosed a resounding sneeze.

"Bless you," Tubby said.

"Thank you," Stuffy and stabbed Tubby in the belly. Tubby weaved back and forth but didn't drop. Blood leaked through his fingers as he gawked at the knife still embedded in his gut.

He opened his mouth to speak but the words wouldn't come.

Sneed Hearn stepped forward to stop Stuffy from eviscerating the bartender but McGoon grabbed Hearn's arm and whispered, "It's too late now."

Impatient at Tubby's refusal to die, Stuffy drew his pistol and fired from two feet away. At that close range, the top of Tubby's head splattered all over the wall, covering the darts in crimson. Tubby dropped like a sack of brass doorknobs. Stuffy yanked the knife out and put it on the bar to wipe the blood off.

He turned to McGoon and said, "That'll learn him. I can't abide —"

Using all of his strength, McGoon hauled back and connected with the right side of Stuffy's jaw. Stuffy went flying backward, flailing his arms uselessly, and crashed into the piano. He sat stunned.

"I'd put a bullet in your brain if I thought

you had one," McGoon said. "You killed a perfectly good bartender."

Stuffy rubbed his swollen jaw and wiped his nose with his sleeve. McGoon added, "You either stop killing on everyone or I swear I'll bury you alive in a ditch. And do something about that snoot of yours — they can hear you all the way to El Paso."

Stuffy responded by letting out a huge sneeze.

"Kill-crazy mutt," McGoon said.

"We best make tracks," Mossy said. "Folks don't cotton to folks killin' other folks, 'specially if they knowed the dead folk. We're gonna be the honored guests at a hangin' party."

"Yeah," said Sneed Hearn. "Sneed not want to be hunged."

McGoon said, "Okay, let's clear out. We'll set up camp down by that creek we passed." He turned to Mossy. "Any witnesses?"

"Just us," Mossy said.

As Stuffy got to his feet — a little unsteadily — he said to McGoon, "I ain't forgettin' this, McGoon. When I get —"

"Shut your stupid mouth," McGoon said, and gave Stuffy a swift boot in the ass, sending him flying through the batwing doors and said, "Half a million outlaws in Texas and I get stuck with the three wise men."

Chapter 16

Exhausted and voraciously hungry, Bailey trudged back to Miss Liddi's boarding house. This evening's bill of fare would be meager at best but Miss Liddi could whip together a five-course meal with only a potato and whatever else was in her larder.

The comet — a word as foreign to him as Latin — was drawing closer with each passing hour. Jedadiah Starkwell had no real idea of when the comet would hit, saying, "Could be a year, could be a month, could be today. Or it could miss Sourwood altogether."

"Sure don't look that way," Doc Cutwater said.

Bailey opened the front door to the boarding house and stepped inside, making sure he wiped his boots on the floor mat first. Things were quiet — all of her lodgers had fled for parts unknown.

"That you, Billy?" Miss Liddi called from

the kitchen.

"Yes'm," he called back, hanging his hat on the rack by the front door.

"Be sure not to track any dirt into the house," she said. "Dinner will be along shortly but first I'd like you to meet our new guest."

"Guest?"

Miss Liddi came out of the kitchen. She was short, squat, and kind of homely at fifty years plus years. But she could work miracles with a frying pan and an ounce of lard.

"Come, Billy, and meet our new guest," she said, taking his arm and guiding him into the dining room. A man sat alone at the table. He stood as they entered.

"Billy, this is our new pastor, Reverend Thornton Goodrich," Miss Liddi said. "He'll be staying with us."

"I am pleased to make your acquaintance, Deputy Marshal Bailey," Goodrich said, extending his hand for a shake.

Bailey took it. Goodrich's handshake was cool and firm.

"Pleased to know you," Bailey said. There was something about this man he instinctively sensed was off. Nothing he could put his finger on, though.

"Now you two sit and jabber while I get

dinner on the table," Miss Liddi said, and disappeared back into the kitchen.

Bailey sat across from Goodrich. The table was set for the usual six or seven lodgers because, as Miss Liddi said, "They might come back."

"What brings you to Sourwood, Reverend Goodrich?" Bailey asked.

"In case you hadn't noticed, sir," Goodrich responded, "the end of creation could very well happen tomorrow. I heard of your former minister's passing and thought the good people of Sourwood could use some spiritual sustenance."

"Aren't as many good people — any people — left in Sourwood," Bailey said. "Half the town has skedaddled, and the other half is hoping for a miracle. I'd say you'll be preaching to the choir but the choir ran away, too."

"Then the ones who remain will need guidance and learn to trust in the Lord, for He has a grand design for humanity."

"And what would that grand design be?"

"Only He knows," Goodrich said. "And the Lord does not *jabber* with his flock."

"You mean you don't know the Lord personally?"

Goodrich eyed the fork on the table six inches away. He wanted to bury it to the hilt into Bailey's neck. He wondered though if it was sharp enough.

Miss Liddi brought out dinner — a platter of boiled potatoes and some dandelion greens.

"Best I could do," she said, a little sheepishly. "Ain't a cow or a chicken to be found anywhere."

"The Lord will provide," Goodrich said.

"If He *is* providing," Bailey said. "If He ain't, I'd say the Good Lord is napping on the job," Bailey said.

"Blasphemy!" Goodrich protested.

Bailey ignored him. "Can the Good Lord at least provide some salt and pepper?"

"Goodness," Miss Liddi said, and went to retrieve them.

Bailey said, "With grub getting harder to find every day, you may regret ever setting foot in Sourwood."

"I go where the Lord needs me," Goodrich said. "I am His servant. And given your food crisis, I'd say this meal looks fit for a king."

"Yeah," Bailey said, "if king is the name of your cocker spaniel."

Goodrich glanced at the fork again. How nice it would look jutting out of this lawman's eyeball.

" *'For He was foreknown before the foundation of the world, but has appeared in these last times for the sake of you.'* Peter, chapter one, verse twenty," Goodrich said. "Are you a true believer, deputy marshal?"

"I believe only what I can see," Bailey said. "Where are you staying while you're in town, Reverend Goodrich?" Bailey asked.

"Why, right here of course," Miss Liddi said as she returned with the salt and pepper. "He'd been planning on boarding in Roscoe Hogg's drafty old cabin but I won't hear of it, not with all the unoccupied rooms I have here."

Bailey felt a knot in his gut.

"I'm not so sure that's a good idea, Miss Liddi," Bailey said, the potatoes forgotten. "Maybe the Reverend would be more comfortable —"

"Oh, pish posh," Miss Liddi said. "I invited him to stay and stay he will, at least until that cursed ball of fire —"

"It's called a comet," Bailey said.

"Until that cursed ball of comet sends us all to meet our Maker," she said, then added, "Well, *most* of us will meet in heaven. Some of us . . . it'll be the other place."

Goodrich smiled at Bailey — there was something sinister in that smile; his black, dead eyes spoke of violence and cold-blooded murder.

"Besides," Miss Liddi said, "be kind of nice having a man of God around, don't you think, Billy?"

"What about that whiskey drummer from St. Louis?" Bailey asked. "He's stopping here, too, isn't he?"

"Yes," Miss Liddi said, "Mr. Quigley, but the poor soul never leaves his room, even at mealtime — it's almost like he isn't here at all."

"Can't blame him for that," Bailey muttered.

Before he could answer, Fendall Harper burst through the front door, sweating like an old sow and half-crazed, eyes wider than silver dollars. "You better get on down to the Saddle Sore, Billy," Fendall said, out of breath. "There's been —" He looked at Miss Liddi, who looked terrified. "Well, just get over there."

Bailey jumped out of his chair and put on his gun and holster, and grabbed his hat before he and Fendall were halfway out the door.

"Maybe I should accompany you," Goodrich offered. "If someone is in need of the Gospel, I —"

"If we need you," Billy said, putting on his holster and jamming his hat on his head, "you'll be the first to know, Preacher."

Chapter 17

Doc Cutwater felt for a pulse, but already knew Stuffy was gone.

"Is he a goner, Doc?" Fendall asked.

"It would appear so," Doc said. "Whoever did this wasn't content to just stab Tubby. Had to shoot into his brain, too."

Billy glanced down at the bloody Barlow on the bar. He picked it up and asked, "This belong to anyone we know?"

Both Fendall and Doc Cutwater shook their heads.

"Start getting a posse together," Bailey told Fendall. "We need to find this rotten apple and stretch his neck."

"A posse?" Fendall asked. "With half the town gone? We ain't got enough men left here for a gin rummy game."

"He's right about that, Billy," Doc Cutwater said. "And besides, the cowardly wretch could be someone in town, maybe a person we see every day. With this comet getting closer by the hour, folks are resigned to their fate and have given up. Some have gone half mad, others full mad."

"But Jed Starkwell said —" Bailey started.

"He said the comet *might* hit Sourwood, or it *might* just pass us by and land on some other town," Doc said. "Either way, with that big ball of hell bearing down, it's hard to keep hoping."

"You ain't just clickin' your teeth, Doc," Fendall said. Which, in Fendall-ese, meant he agreed with Doc's prognosis.

Billy sighed. He wished that darn comet would land and get it over with once and for all.

"I still owed him three dollars," Fendall said, holding back tears.

CHAPTER 18

Sneed Hearn managed to bag a mangy old rabbit so at least there'd be some meat for supper. Not much — it was a pretty skinny rabbit — but better than nothing. Mossy was trying to skin it with not much success. His knife was dull and rusty. He had stoked the fire in preparation of roasting the bunny.

They were camped by the creek and not surprisingly, McGoon wasn't too concerned about any posse. Truth was, knowing their days were numbered, most people in Sourwood gave up caring about anything.

Stuffy was knee-deep in the creek, trying to knock a trout senseless with a big tree branch. He kept slapping on the water like he was mad at it.

"Fish are smarter than he is," Mossy said as they watched the comic spectacle.

"You just figuring that out?" McGoon asked.

"Hey, Stuffy," Mossy called out. "Let me

borrow your pig sticker. Mine ain't worth spit."

"My what?" Stuffy called back.

"Your pig sticker," Mossy said again.

"What the heck is a pig sticker?" Stuffy asked.

"A pig sticker, a *knife,* peckerhead. He wants to borrow your knife."

"Then why didn't he say so," Stuffy grumbled. He was in a bad mood — he hadn't caught a single fish. He walked back to the camp, reaching down to his sheath for the knife, but it wasn't there.

Then, the realization hit him like a punch in the head — he'd left it at the Saddle Sore saloon.

"Lost it, didn't you?" McGoon said, looking very unhappy.

"I didn't losc it, not exactly," Stuffy said. "I know where it is —"

"So do I," McGoon said. "You left it at the damned saloon, didn't you?"

"What if I did?" Stuffy said, getting hot and flustered. "Not like anyone knows it's mine."

"I disagree," McGoon said. "Your loving devotion to shooting and stabbing anyone unfortunate enough to cross your bloody path has got the law hunting us like rabid dogs. And they'll know the knife is yours, dumbhead. You might as well have carved your name on it."

"Who carves their name on a knife?" Mossy asked.

McGoon ignored him. Stuffy said, clearly shaken, "What should I do?"

"I'll tell you what you're gonna do, pickle-brain," McGoon said. "You're gonna ride back to that saloon and fetch that knife. And don't come back till you do."

McGoon had killed men for less, Stuffy knew. He saddled his horse and mounted up. "What if someone sees me or catches me? They'll hang me for sure."

"If they do," McGoon said, slapping the horse's rump to get him moving, "it will prove once and for all that there really is a God."

Sourwood was almost a ghost town, Stuffy thought as he trotted down the main street. All the houses and businesses were dark, save for a few windows where weak lantern light flickered.

The streets were deserted. Stuffy brought his horse to a halt in front of the Saddle Sore and tied it to the hitching post. The Saddle Sore was dark and deserted. He made his way to the saloon where he'd left the knife.

Problem was, the knife wasn't there. Stuffy looked down the length of the bar. No knife.

Stuffy felt the cold metal of a shotgun barrel on the back of his neck.

"Move and I'll shoot you right in the sweetmeats," came Fendall's voice. "You trash."

Bailey popped up from behind the bar, holding the knife.

"Looking for this?" he asked the outlaw.

CHAPTER 19

"Hands over your head," Fendall said. Stuffy complied.

"You killed Tubby Nooner, an old pal, and probably the best bartender in the territory," Bailey said, wanting to rip this murderer's head clean off. "Why?"

"I didn't murder nobody," Stuffy said. Fendall prodded Stuffy's neck with the shotgun.

"Tubby's lying dead in Doc Cutwater's tool shed," Bailey said, "and he ain't getting any fresher."

"You'd be wise to answer the man's question," Fendall said.

"You can go kiss a rattlesnake's ass," Stuffy said.

Bailey shook his head in mock sadness, saying, "Our friend here has a wicked tongue, Fendall. Why don't you teach him some manners."

Fendall brought the shotgun down hard

on Stuffy's head. He staggered for a moment, then dropped and went face down onto the sawdust-covered barroom floor.

"Varmint has hisself a hard head," Fendall remarked.

"Let's tie him up and drag this lowlife back to the jail," Bailey said.

"Can I shoot him first?" Fendall asked.

"Tempting as it may sound," Bailey said, "he just might be worth more alive. I got to ride over to the Starkwell ranch, see if Jed knows anything more. Can you handle this scum?"

For an older man, Fendall was still strong. He slung an unconscious Stuffy over his shoulder, and said, "It'll be joy in the morning when we stretch his neck."

"Throw him into a cell," Bailey said. "And don't be gentle."

Bailey mounted up and galloped down Main Street. Fendall made his way to the jail, Stuffy's muttering was broken by an occasional sneeze.

"Don't you be gittin' nose jam all over me," Fendall said.

Though his wrists were bound together, Stuffy somehow managed to grab his knife from Fendall's back pocket and thrust it into Fendall's ass. Not deep but enough to get his attention. Fendall howled and dropped face-first onto the dusty street. Stuffy seized the opportunity to leap to his feet and scampered away like a jack rabbit.

Fendall patted his rump — some blood but not much; the knife hadn't gone in that deep. He got to his feet and started chasing after Stuffy.

Stuffy ran full speed down the alleyway between the Mervin Milgrim's blacksmith shop and the café and out onto another street. He ran toward a small house. His hands were still bound together so he kicked the front door open, and darted into the first room he came to. He kicked that door open as well. The name plate on the door said "Primm."

The first thing he saw was an ancient old lady, sitting up in bed and aiming an 1820 U.S. military flintlock straight at Stuffy's chest.

"Ravage me, will ya, you lowlife bottom-feeder?" Hortense Primm growled.

Stuffy said, "I don't —" and sneezed. Miss Hortense shot him. Once, she could shoot anything she could see but at her advanced age, her aim was a little off. The bullet took off most of Stuffy's right ear. He howled.

"Serves you right!" Miss Hortense said, and fired again. The shot went wild and shattered the bedroom window. "And don't even think about doing anything with that flapdoodle between your legs."

The gunshots would attract the attention of that old duffer Fendall. Stuffy turned tail and ran out of the house, hearing Miss Hortense bellow, "Ain't a soul alive who'll have at me, no sir! I'll kill him dead!"

Stuffy practically dived out the front door again and zigzagged down one street then another until he found himself right back on Main Street. Fendall was rounding the alleyway. Stuffy started running again.

He spotted an open door under a sign that said "Milligan Sartorial Parlor." Stuffy darted inside, saw a fat, balding man sat dozing in the barber chair. Still moving, Stuffy glanced at the ceiling-high piles of dirt. He tripped over a hunk of lumber and fell head-first onto what was now referred to as Milligan's Hole.

Stuffy hit the water hard. He sputtered and spit out the muddy water and then sneezed three times in a row.

"One to a customer," Fendall said, peering into the hole. Stuffy was covered with mud and some blood mixed in.

Lomax Milligan awakened suddenly. He said, "Everything okay, Fendall?"

"Peachy keen," Fendall said.

"How about getting me the hell out of

here?" Stuffy said. "I've already got —" He sneezed, "— one foot in the grave."

"One ain't enough," Fendall said.

"Who is that?" Milligan was curious.

"The man who kilt Tubby Nooner," Fendall said.

Chapter 20

"Heaven is on fire!"

Thornton Goodrich clutched the Good Book against his chest. He was dressed for work — black hat, long, black greatcoat, starched white shirt, and floppy black necktie. Despite the searing heat, the man didn't appear to be sweating even a drop.

He was standing on the back of an old buckboard. He was preaching to the wind but the faithful would show up before long. They always did.

"In Daniel, Chapter twelve, verse three, it is written 'and the Almighty spoke to Daniel, who said, As for me, I heard but could not understand; My Lord, what will be the outcome of these events?' And the Almighty said, 'Do not be afraid, Daniel, for from the first day that you set your heart on understanding this and on humbling yourself before Me, your words were heard, and I have come in response to your words . . . O

Daniel, man of high esteem, understand the words that I am about to tell you and stand upright, for I have now been sent to you."

Standing in the plank sidewalk outside the jail, Fendall said to Bailey, "This is getting good. What happens next? What does the Lord say?"

"I dunno," Bailey said. "But he's preaching to the choir."

"What choir?" Fendall asked. "Ain't no choir here to sing."

"The Almighty Himself talked of a future time so horrendous that no human lives would be spared 'unless those days were shortened' — Matthew, Chapter 24, verse 22," Goodrich intoned.

A few people gathered to listen.

"Seven!" Goodrich said. "Seven is the number of completeness. And the Lord desires that we come completely out of any kind of sinful life we may be involved with, and no longer serve sin. No longer be a slave to sin, to completely come out of sin. And early on the eighth day, the fire in the heavens will roar with death and destruction and this town, this Sourwood, will perish from the face of the earth."

The crowd was growing larger. Mrs. Alma Swayzee, who taught Sunday school, fainted dead away.

"Did he just say what I think he said?" Bailey asked.

"I think that's what he said," Fendall replied.

It wasn't unusual for these circuit riders to get all wrathy and fired up when preaching to the unbelievers, but this Goodrich was taking the Gospel to new, terrifying heights.

"But it does not have to be this way — if you repent! Yes, repent. In Matthew, Chapter four, verse seventeen, it is written, 'Repent, change your inner self — your old way of thinking, regret past sins, live your life in a way that proves repentance; seek God's purpose, for the kingdom of heaven is at hand.'

"Repent and be baptized every one of you in the name of the Good Lord for the forgiveness of your sins, and you will receive the most precious gift of all — your mortal souls."

A dozen or more people had gathered to listen, then more came, mostly out of curiosity.

"Man's a real silver-tongue spellbinder, ain't he?" Fendall said.

"In Luke, chapter thirteen verse three, it says 'unless you repent, you will all likewise perish. James, Chapter four verse eight, speaks 'Draw near to the Almighty, and He will draw near to you. Cleanse your hands, you sinners, and purify your hearts!' "

"Praise the Lord!" someone — it sounded like Short Stack — bellowed, and a few others chimed in.

"In our spiritual journey," Goodrich said, "it is vital to be aware of the signs of the End. The scriptures tell us that certain events will unfold as the world approaches its conclusion. We may notice these signs in current events around us, but rather than being filled with dread, we should feel a sense of anticipation and alertness. The Almighty's word invites us to prepare our hearts and minds, remaining vigilant in faith as we witness these signs. Together, let us explore what the Bible says, always knowing that God's love protects us through uncertain times.

"Seven days," Goodrich went on. "Seven days . . . and on the eighth, Judgment Day is at hand. If you want to roast in the fires of Hell, so be it, for you shall. You must repent to enjoy all the blessings of Heaven."

"Blessings?" Fendall asked. "Man just said Heaven was on fire."

"A figure of speech," Bailey said.

"Oh," Fendall said. "Guess I was taking him illiterately."

Bailey went back inside where Stuffy was sliding in and out of consciousness, thanks in large part to the healthy slug of laudanum Doc Cutwater had given him when patching him up. A large ribbon of gauze was wrapped around his head, another around the fleshy lump of skin that had formerly been his right ear.

Stuffy stirred but did not awaken. He'd be of no use, information-wise, for five more hours. Bailey went back outside to watch Goodrich waving his fist at the sky and screaming about balls of fire raining down from the heavens and turning Sourwood into one big barbeque.

Bailey was very surprised when he saw Agnes Jean and her Aunt Tinky in the crowd. On closer examination, it looked like Aunt Tinky was forcefully dragging Agnes Jean into the crowd. They were a distance away but Bailey could hear Aunt Tinky's big mouth.

"You're going to listen to this man of God or I'll know the reason why," Aunt Tinky screamed.

Bailey saw Agnes Jean say something to Aunt Tinky, who responded, "Listen up, girl — this man may be our only hope! He is close to the Lord."

Agnes Jean spoke louder now, saying, "A

mud puddle is closer to the Lord than *Reverend* Goodrich."

"Shut your filthy mouth and listen — he says we have to repent to save our souls," Aunt Tinky said.

"Our souls?" Agnes Jean said. "What good is a soul without a body to go with it?"

"Blasphemy!" Aunt Tinky shrieked.

"Shrew!" Agnes Jean snapped back. She'd never even remotely come close to calling her Aunt Tinky a shrew.

Enraged, Aunt Tinky gave her niece a healthy slap in the face. Agnes Jean slapped her back, something else she'd never dreamed of doing. And darned if it didn't feel pretty good.

Goodrich stopped preaching — he couldn't take his eyes off Agnes Jean, prettiest girl in this Godforsaken town. True, there were only a few women in Sourwood who'd be of use to anyone, but this gal would look good in a burlap sack.

Bailey ran into the crowd, who wisely gave Agnes Jean and her Aunt Tinky plenty of room to have it out.

"Been waiting years for Agnes Jean to wake up and smell the coffee," said one man in the crowd.

Bailey tore them apart before the punching and hair-pulling could start.

"Calm down, Aggie," Bailey said.

"Why don't you mind your own business?" Aunt Tinky said. "You tinhorn tosspot!"

"Don't talk to my fiancé like that!" Agnes Jean snapped.

"Your what?" Aunt Tinky wanted to know. "Your *what*?"

"The man I'm going to marry, that's what," Agnes Jean said. "And you can't stop me."

"You'll not marry *him,*" Aunt Tinky said, motioning toward Bailey. "The man you'll marry will be respectable."

"Why do you dislike me so much?" Bailey asked, though the truth was, he no longer seemed to care one way or the other.

Aunt Tinky ignored him. Fendall grabbed Bailey by the arm and led him a few yards away.

"You didn't know Miss Tinky and your father were all biblical together after your mother died," Fendall said.

"My father and Miss Tinky were —"

"Yes," Fendall said. "At least four, sometimes five times a week. Tinky thought he'd ask her to marry him but he never did."

"Why didn't you tell me this before Agnes Jean and I became engaged?"

"Engaged?" Fendall said. "You ain't even

given her one of them engagement rings."

"Don't change the subject," Bailey said.

"Broke Tinky's heart, your daddy did," Fendall said. "And none of us was even sure she had one."

This was a new and unexpected wrinkle. Bailey said, "I'll ask you again — why was I never told?"

"Because your daddy swore me to silence," Fendall said. "He tried to keep it a secret but small towns like Sourwood, one man's secret is everybody's business. So your daddy stopped seeing Tinky — didn't seem fittin' for the town marshal to be carrying on like he were."

"Well, prairie oysters on fire and save the matches," Bailey muttered.

Meanwhile, Agnes Jean and Aunt Tinky were still going at it.

"Washing, ironing, cooking for you till my fingers bled," Aunt Tinky said. "You always had clean clothes and a full belly."

"And I suppose that gave you the right to dominate me, belittle me, make me feel useless and unwanted," Agnes Jean said.

"I took you in when you were knee high to a bumble bee," Aunt Tinky said.

"It's 'knee-high to a grasshopper'," Agnes Jean said.

With that, she spun on her heels and

headed back to Aunt Tinky's house.

"Where are you going?" Aunt Tinky asked.

"Home —"

"*My* home," Aunt Tinky said.

"*Our* home," Agnes Jean said. "Or have you forgotten that my parents bought and paid for the house provided you take me in should something happen to them. And sadly, it did!"

She turned and started walking again.

"Pack your things and quick — you are no longer welcome in *my* house."

"If that big fat comet doesn't destroy us all, we'll let the bank decide who really owns that house," Agnes Jean said. "They still have all the paperwork."

She continued on home, saying, "And if you need me — I don't know why you would since you never did before — I'll be lodging at Miss Liddiflower's boarding house!"

Bailey said, "Aggie, please —"

"You shut up, too," she said, and kicked him in the leg.

Still standing on the buckboard, Goodrich smiled.

I'll be lodging at Miss Liddiflower's boarding house.

You must shower that pretty lady with love and sympathy, Goodrich thought. Sympathy first, then love. Lots of it.

Aunt Tinky, ready to spit bullets, waved a fist at Bailey and said, "This is all your fault, you weasel!"

"What did I do?" Bailey asked, getting a little warm under the collar.

Aunt Tinky responded by punching him in the belly, almost knocking the breath out of him. He bent over, clutching his stomach.

"One day you're the king of the hill, the next day you're buried under it," he heard Fendall say.

He also heard Reverend Goodrich who was saying now, "But about that day or hour no one knows, not even the angels in heaven, nor the Son, but only the Father. Then will appear the sign of the Son of Man in heaven. And then all the peoples of the earth will mourn when they see the Son of Man coming on the clouds of heaven! And He will send His angels with a loud trumpet call, and they will gather in Him from the four winds, from one end of the heavens to the other. Listen, a noise on the mountains — the Lord Almighty is mustering an army for war. They come from faraway lands, from the ends of the heavens — the Lord and the weapons of his wrath — to destroy the whole world in a great big ball of fire . . . And He will send His angels with a loud trumpet call, and they will gather in Him from the four winds, from one end of the heavens to the other!"

Goodrich had Bailey's friends and neighbors all riled up. They were frightened enough with the way things were going.

Bailey didn't like it one bit.

Chapter 21

Goodrich stepped down off the buckboard. Leaning against it was a tough looking hombre — Goodrich couldn't recall seeing him in Sourwood before. The man was chewing a toothpick.

The man said to Goodrich, "You really believe that hogwash mumbo jumbo you're spouting, Reverend? Now me, I'd take it with about two million grains of salt."

"I don't believe we've been introduced," Goodrich said. It was dawning on him that he knew this stranger from somewhere. "I am Thornton Goodrich, here to spread the good word about —"

"Cut the twaddle," the man said. "You're Calvin Culpepper. Thrown out of West Point for slashing three classmates with a machete." McGoon shook his head. "Clearly, you don't play well with other children, Mr. Culpepper. Made quite a name for yourself since then, haven't you? Spied for the Confederacy, spied for the Union till both sides wanted to see you dancing on the end of a rope . . . Peddled captive gringo women to slave traders in Ciudad Acuna — but not before you tried them out for size. Sold guns to the Comancheria, cattle rustling . . . you even rode with Sam Bass and the Collins Brothers gang, too — a bloodthirsty bunch, weren't they? Shall I continue?"

"I'm afraid you have me at a disadvantage, sir," Goodrich said. "I am an ordained minister —"

"You're an ordained lunatic," McGoon said. "With half of the Texas Rangers lookin' for you."

"You must have mistaken me for someone else," Goodrich said.

McGoon said, "You're just lucky the Rangers got bigger fish to fry these days, what with the end of the world and such. Is it really seven days till that big rock lands on our noggins?"

"You doubtless heard my sermon," Goodrich said. "To which I say, draw your own conclusions."

"Have it your way," McGoon said. "I'm a wanted man myself."

"For what, stealing an apple pie off a windowsill?"

"Draw your own conclusions, Mr. Culpepper," McGoon said. "Maybe I'll see you around." With that, he walked off into the dusk.

There was a small window in the jail cell where Stuffy sat, shackled to the bunk with a three-foot chain to an ankle cuff.

There were bars on the small window though they hardly seemed necessary — it was about eighteen inches by eighteen inches; even a dwarf couldn't squeeze through.

Stuffy was about to doze off when he heard, "Stuffy! Stuffy!"

He responded by sneezing three times.

"Who's that?"

"It's me, Dex," came the response.

"Dex who?" Stuffy asked.

"McGoon, you horse's ass," Stuffy heard him say. "Go to the window."

Stuffy dutifully scrambled off the bunk, forgetting the chain around his ankle. He managed to take two steps before it tightened — he fell backwards onto the floor with a thud that sent ripples of pain up his spine.

"I cain't," Stuffy said. "They got me hogtied to the bunk. When are you gonna get me out of here? They're fixin' to execulate me!"

"That's 'execute,' " McGoon corrected.

Earlier that day, Bailey brought him a lunch of bony catfish and some kind of mush.

Hungry as he was, Stuffy descended on the meal like a bunch of crows. As he ate, he said to Bailey, "I don't know much, but I do know I'm supposed to have a trial with a jury."

"You are indeed," Bailey said. "But given the situation, we're pressed for time so we had the trial while you were sleeping."

Stuffy felt a momentary glimmer of hope. He asked, "How'd I do?"

"Not too well," Bailey said. "We brought you in guilty. Execution's tomorrow at sun-up. That is, if the comet don't turn us all into dust."

"I didn't see no gallows," Stuffy protested.

"No, you don't," Bailey said. "And we ain't got time to build one, either, which is why I'm taking the liberty of shooting you in the head."

"Is that legal?" Stuffy asked.

"Does it matter?"

"I guess not," Stuffy said.

"You may want to make your peace with the Almighty while you can," Bailey said. "Considering He appears to have a lot on His mind. You like, I can send for that

Reverend Goodrich to stop by and mumble a few prayers for your everlasting soul."

Now, McGoon was standing on a wooden crate so he could see in. He felt no affection for Stuffy Grandstaff, no remorse at the thought of him being put to death.

"So you gonna spring me from this pig pen before dawn?" Stuffy wanted to know. "That marshal said he'd put a bullet in my brain."

"It'll take that bullet a week to find it," McGoon said.

"I don't wanna die, Dex," Stuffy said. "There's no future in it."

"Don't worry, jughead. Nobody's gonna kill you before I get the chance," McGoon said. "Sit tight — let me study on this."

"Study fast, okay?" Stuffy said.

Chapter 22

"I was wondering," Doc Cutwater said to Thornton Goodrich, "if you'd be so kind enough to drop in on Matilda Gallagher and see if you can offer any comfort in her time of need."

"What seems to be ailing her?" Goodrich asked, already knowing the answer.

"Matilda's husband Axel never came home from some Rock Springs. Left over a week ago, was supposed to only be gone two days. Poor Matilda's at wit's end with worry. Maybe you can give her some biblical quotations to ease her fears a little."

Goodrich was atop the buckboard, spit-shining his shoes. He said, "Poor soul. Has anyone tried to find him? Maybe he ran off — another woman, perhaps."

"I don't think so," Doc said. "Matilda ain't the sharpest tool in the shed but she's very easy on the eyes, if you know what I mean. Man would have to be plumb loco to run out on her."

"My first commitment is to my new congregation," Goodrich said. "Of course I will drop in on her. The Good Lord put me here to comfort those in need of repentance."

Doc Cutwater wanted to cringe — like Bailey, there was something about this preacher that didn't sit right, kind of like the undercooked liver and onions from the café.

"I don't think Matilda's in need of repenting," Doc said. "She just wants her husband back. As for me, I admittedly fear the worst."

"You display a lack of faith, sir," Goodrich said. "Perhaps if you prayed . . ."

"No disrespect, Reverend," Doc said, "but sometimes — and I think today qualifies — faith and prayer just ain't enough."

"I understand, Doctor," Goodrich said, wondering how long Doc Cutwater would live with a Mexican deluxe gentleman's dagger embedded between his shoulder blades.

Goodrich borrowed a horse from Short Stack Barlow, and using Doc's directions, made his way to the Gallagher ranch.

He'd been expecting a weary, wind-blown, skinny old hag like many homely frontier wives, whose faces could be used as live bait. Matilda Gallagher was quite attractive.

Thirty-one, maybe thirty-two at most. Her pretty face was angelic, almost mesmerizing, surprising given the rough life of a rancher's missus. Even clad in her baggy overalls and her hair tied into a severe bun, there was something unmistakably sensuous about her. Her breasts were firm and upright, struggling to escape the confines of her tight work shirt.

In other words, a gal who inspired deviant fantasies without trying.

The Gallagher ranch house was a little weather-beaten, as many houses in Texas were — rain, wind, and the almost constant heat had taken their toll. A few coats of paint would have worked wonders

Miss Matilda was sweeping the porch steps when Goodrich rode up. She gave him a nice, friendly Texas welcome, saying, "Whatever you're selling, we don't need any."

Goodrich dismounted and said, "I'm afraid you have mistaken me for someone else, Miss Gallagher. I am the Reverend Thornton Goodrich."

"You could be the president of France, it wouldn't matter none," Matilda said. "I ain't looking to buy any more bibles, if that's what you're selling."

"I'm not selling anything, Miss," Goodrich said. "Doctor Cutwater thought I may be of some spiritual help to you in this, your hour of need."

She leaned the broom up against the screen door. "Doc Cutwater sent you, did he?"

"He did indeed," Goodrich said, his gaze fixated on her breasts. "May I come in?"

"I've seen a few saddle preachers around the territory but I don't recall meeting you," she said.

"I was asked to spread the gospel after the untimely passing of Reverend Broadhurst."

"That tired old coot," she said, "couldn't find sin in a Fort Worth cathouse." Then she asked, "This got anything to do with Axel not coming home?"

"Yes, it does," Goodrich said.

"And what about that big hunk of rock in the sky, gonna turn us all into cinders? You got any thoughts on that?"

"As I matter of fact, I do," Goodrich said. "If I may enter your home I will share my thoughts with you."

"Can't you share 'em where you're standing?"

"I suppose so," Goodrich said, "but that would hardly be charitable. I've come here in all good faith."

Matilda grasped the doorknob to the house. She turned to ask, "You ain't got any fancy notions about baptizing me?"

"The Lord put me on this earth to give aid and comfort to those in need," he said. "I'm not here to drown you in the creek."

"Good, cause I cain't swim," Matilda said, opening the door and going inside. Goodrich followed her.

She still wasn't sure of this preacher's intentions. She knew what drove the lusts of men and the effect she had on them — she knew she was very pretty. And Doc Cutwater, the only man in Sourwood with a brain larger than a peanut, *did* send him after all.

Matilda pulled out a chair from the kitchen table and said, "Sit, Preacher."

Goodrich sat. Matilda said, "I'd offer you coffee or tea but I'm plumb out of both. Ever since that thing appeared in the sky, nothing's been coming through." She thought for a moment and added, "Got some acorn juice I could warm up."

"No, thank you, Miss Matilda," Goodrich said.

She sat down opposite him at the table. He wasn't a bad looking man, not shabby and caked with trail dust like most circuit riders. No, this one was pretty clean and had the look of someone who actually cared about his appearance.

It was his sparkling cold-blue eyes that gave Matilda pause.

"Axel's dead, ain't he?" she asked.

"You don't know that, not at all," Goodrich said.

"Like I told Billy Bailey, the town marshal, it ain't natural for Axel to not come home.

"Maybe he . . . maybe Mr. Gallagher met another woman."

"Not hardly," Matilda said. "Axel don't eat meat scraps on the trail when he's got sirloin steak at home. No sir, something bad happened to him."

Despite her best efforts not to, Matilda found herself attracted to this preacher man. Most circuit riders were girl-crazy, and more than few frontier wives ran off with them. And Axel, fifteen years older than Matilda, had been having problems fulfilling his husbandly duties of late, leaving them both quite frustrated. Matilda more so. Her stomach was all fluttery, like she'd swallowed a hummingbird.

"I'm sure," Goodrich said, rising to his feet, "that Mr. Gallagher will come waltzing through that door very soon."

He stood behind her at the table and put his hands on her shoulders, saying, "After all, what man in his right mind would leave a beautiful lady such as yourself?"

He massaged her shoulders. Matilda instinctively flinched but this preacher's hands were magic.

"You shouldn't ought to be doing this," she said, shaking his hands away.

"It is merely a way to help you relax," he said.

"I cain't relax knowing there's a gun on your hip," she said. "What's a preacher doing with a gun?"

"Not everyone on the frontier is brimming with Christian charity," he said, and pulled the gun from the holster. He set it down on the kitchen table.

Matilda looked at it, asking, "Is that by any chance a Colt Navy revolver?"

Goodrich cursed himself for being so darn ignorant. He'd meant to leave the Colt in his saddlebags.

"I guess it is," he said. "You know your weaponry, don't you?"

"Where'd you get it?" she asked.

"I don't quite recall," Goodrich said, moving away from her. "Why do you ask?"

"Because it's Axel's gun, that's why," she said, snatching the Colt from the table and pointing it at his head, cocking the trigger.

"There must be some mistake," he said, and didn't believe it himself.

"Axel is never without that gun," Matilda said. "Heck, he even takes it with him when he goes to the outhouse."

"Miss Matilda —"

"For shootin' rats, he says. And speaking of rats, what did you do to my Axel?"

"I never met the man," Goodrich said. "As the Lord is my witness, I have no knowledge of him or his whereabouts."

"You're a lowdown lying dog," Matilda said, and pulled the trigger.

There was a dry click. She fired again with the same results.

"Could have told you it wasn't loaded," Goodrich said. Matilda pulled the trigger again, and this time the Colt fired. The bullet went wild and slammed into a framed wedding portrait of the happy couple when they tied the knot.

Goodrich moved swiftly and slapped the Colt out of her hand. "You crazy fool," he said, hauling off and giving her a punch in the face that sent her sprawling.

Goodrich towered over her. Matilda whimpered as he took off his belt.

"Yes, I killed your precious Axel. I ripped him from gullet to gizzard and watched his guts run out into the dirt, an early breakfast for the vultures," he said.

"You miserable son of a bi—"

"Now, now, Miss Matilda," Goodrich said, twirling his belt. "No obscenities in my presence, please — I am a servant of the Lord."

"What are you gonna do to me?" Matilda asked, cowering in fear, just the way Goodrich liked 'em.

"Whatever tickles my fancy, little lady, whatever tickles my fancy."

Chapter 23

Short, stocky, and balding at the tender age of thirty, Eldon Quigley was a whiskey drummer out of St. Louis, the Paroo Brothers Distillery ("Finest Spirituous and Malt Liquors and Wines in the West"). Sourwood was supposed to be his last stop in this part of Texas, scheduled as he was to take the Livermore & Beedle Stagecoach line back to Dallas and, ultimately, home.

Problem was, the stagecoach never showed up per the schedule — this was more than a week ago and none of Livermore and Beedle's stages had come through. Like everyone else, Quigley was terrified. With no place to go and no way to get there even if he did, it looked like Eldon Quigley was going to meet his Maker in this wretched one-horse town.

Holed up in his room at Miss Liddi's, Quigley took to his bed with only his suitcase filled with bottles of hooch from

Livermore and Beedle. Folks in town, had they known about Quigley's stash of whiskey, wouldn't even stop short of killing him to get their greasy hands on it.

So instead, Quigley hoarded the twenty bottles, determined to drink himself to death before he was turned roasted into a few gray cinders. It *was* possible for a man to end it all by pouring whiskey down his gullet. He'd read about it in some magazine. He'd drink, pass out and expire, and all his worries would be gone.

The irony was, Eldon Quigley never touched the stuff. Until now.

Quigley drank discreetly in his room, day and night. Even in a perpetual state of an alcoholic fog, though, he was still terrified.

There was a preacher man who'd just shown up and was occupying the room next door. Though not a religious man, Quigley, thought it couldn't hurt to confess his sins to a holy man and, while he was at it, ask the holy man to have a word with the Almighty about the impending doom. Maybe it wasn't going to happen, maybe the Lord had a change of heart. Maybe . . .

Quigley knew he was deluding himself — that ball of ever-lasting fire was headed right for Sourwood and nothing could stop it.

But a little confab with that Reverend

Goodrich. Seemed like a nice enough fella.

Quigley roused himself, splashed cold water on his face, combed his hair and put on the last clean shirt he had. Wouldn't be fitting to greet a preacher in clothes that looked like he'd slept in them, which in fact he had.

Before the left the room, he realized it was impolite to come empty-handed so he grabbed the last bottle of whisky in his suitcase. As a present. And why not? Even a saddle preacher would welcome a nip or two when Sourwood, Texas, was staring down an apocalypse.

What could it hurt?

Quigley checked himself in the mirror one last time, then started downstairs. He got to the third step, weaving unsteadily — he was drunker than he thought. His eyes rolled up into his head like the symbols on a one-armed bandit. He folded up and pitched forward, tumbling ass over teakettle and ended up on the bottom of the stairwell. The bottle of whiskey had miraculously survived the fall unbroken, lying next to Quigley.

Miss Liddi, who'd been reading the Montgomery Ward catalogue — she needed a new bustle — heard the commotion from the living room. She found the drummer motionless on the floor, his arms and legs twisted in almost comical positions. At that moment the Reverend Goodrich arrived back at the boarding house.

"What in the name of all that's holy happened here?" he asked, looking down at the tangled heap that had once been Eldon Quigley.

"Mr. Quigley," Miss Liddi said, all aflutter. "He never used the handrail."

Goodrich squatted down to take a closer took. Quigley wasn't breathing. His face was whiter than calves milk, lifeless eyes still partially open.

"Is he . . . dead?" she asked.

"Looks that way," Goodrich said. "Lord, he smells like a distillery."

"Goodness!" Miss Liddi exclaimed. "I must go get Doctor Cutwater at once."

"He needs an undertaker, not a doctor," Goodrich said.

"We don't have one," Miss Liddi said, and flew out the front door and down the street to Doc Cutwater's office.

Goodrich picked up the bottle of whiskey and took a swig. Quigley hawked the best rotgut in the territory.

"Holding out on us, eh, Mr. Quigley?"

He didn't wait for an answer. He went out the front door, clutching the bottle, and saw candlelight flickering in Sturdley's mercantile window.

He looked up — the burning ball of death and destruction was bearing down, closer still than a day earlier. In his fiery sermon, he'd said seven days till Purgatory but now, on day three, they might not have to wait that long.

He looked in the window and just happened to notice three nuggets of what looked very much like gold sitting next to Sturdley's cashbox, which was likely empty.

He went into the mercantile — Sturdley had stopped locking the door, as there was little left to buy or steal.

He was fast asleep behind the counter, obviously in the throes of a very pleasant dream.

"Oh, Miss Cecilia . . . do that again . . . oh, Miss Cecilia . . . lower this time . . . do me right . . ."

Goodrich banged his fist on the counter, rousing Sturdley, who blinked and shook his head to clear it.

"Reverend?" he asked.

"Who's Miss Cecilia?" Goodrich asked.

"Miss Cecilia?" Sturdley asked.

"The Miss Cecilia you were dreaming about."

Sturdley grinned slightly and said, "Oh,

she were a working gal I met over to New Braunfels, had her a body made for sin . . ." Sturdley realized what he was saying.

"None of your beeswax," he said to Goodrich. "Don't be a nosy Nellie."

"I meant no harm," Goodrich said.

"What can I do for you, Reverend? If you come in to buy something, I probably ain't got any."

Goodrich put the bottle of whiskey on the counter. "I seek nothing, sir, but some intelligent conversation and perhaps a little liquid refreshment?"

"Where'd you get that whiskey?" Sturdley asked. "Town's been dryer than Death Valley in August."

"Oh, it was a gift from the late Eldon Quigley."

Sturdley asked, "Did you say the *late* Eldon Quigley, that weasel whiskey drummer?"

"I'm afraid so," Goodrich said. "The poor soul has sadly gone to meet his maker."

"Meaning . . . what exactly?"

"Mr. Quigley was imbibing his own product and fell down the stairs of the boarding house."

"That's too bad," Sturdley said.

"Yes, indeed it is," Goodrich. "May I ask you, sir — would that be gold over there?"

Sturdley picked up one of the nuggets. "Well . . . yes. Some folks use it to settle their bill."

"I see," Goodrich said. "May I ask who gave you this gold?"

"Well, I'm not supposed to say — it's what they call 'confidential.' Means, don't tell no one."

"Of course," Goodrich said. "Please pardon my curiosity."

"Anyway, ain't nobody knows where it's buried."

"Must be someone who knows," Goodrich said. "Perhaps the very one who buried it?"

"I think I've said about as much as I ought to," Sturdley said.

Goodrich pushed the bottle of hooch toward the merchant. "Would you care for a little libation, Mr. Sturdley?"

Before he could answer, Dex McGoon appeared out of the shadows where the farm implements were kept. He was chewing on a toothpick.

"Let's all have a libation," he said.

Goodrich didn't look too happy to see McGoon. He said, "Well, bless my soul in the bosom of Abraham."

"I can't speak for Abraham," McGoon said, "nor his bosom, but I could sure use a drink of whatever's in that bottle."

Goodrich lifted the bottle, about to drink, when McGoon grabbed the preacher's wrist, and not gently. For a moment, Goodrich looked stunned.

McGoon said, "Now where are your manners, Reverend? Our gracious host here, Mr. Sturdley, should take the first swig."

He pushed the bottle toward Sturdley, who hoisted it and took a nice long drink.

"I'm obliged," Sturdley said, and handed the bottle back to McGoon.

McGoon shook his head, saying, "Oh, have another, sir — it's the least we can do to show our gratitude."

Gratitude for what? Sturdley thought, but gladly accepted the offer anyway. The second swig went down much more easily.

He knew these men were likely not to be trusted but his thirst outweighed his better judgment.

McGoon offered him a third swig. Sturdley happily accepted. He was getting happy all over.

Chapter 24

"You really kilt twenty-two people?" Fendall asked.

"Give or take," Stuffy said from the jail cell. Fendall had removed the cuffs — the little rat they called Stuffy wasn't going anywhere.

Fendall sat in the marshal's chair with the rifle across his lap. He asked, "Give or take?"

"Might've been twenty-two if you include my grandpa," Stuffy said, and sneezed twice.

"You slaughtered your own kin?"

"Had it coming, the old buzzard," Stuffy said.

"Why?" Fendall was getting curious now.

"He wasn't really my kin," Stuffy said. "He was a slimy old crud named Alvin Sanders, who took me in after my mama — she was a whore in Hell's Half Acre — got beat to death by some liquored-up cowboy."

Fendall listened.

"For the price of burying my mama in an unmarked grave, he got hisself a young slave. Worked me almost to death, baling hay, harvesting crops, digging a well, shearing the sheep, plucking the feathers off chickens, chopping up firewood, everything. If I didn't finish a chore, he beat me till I was bleeding out of my nose and mouth. Sometimes he used his buggy whip on me, odd since he didn't have a buggy. Then, just to make sure I learned my lesson, he starved me for days at a time. That jaw-flapping, yellow-bellied bottom feeder did nothing but watch me break my back in the fields while he sat on his big ass and drank that rotgut tarantula juice he cooked up in the barn."

"Sounds like a real peach," Fendall said.

Stuffy continued, "He taught me how to be evil."

"And here I thought it came to you all natural-like."

"Then when I was still a kid, twelve maybe, I was chopping wood for the cookstove when Mr. Alvin, drunk as a skunk, started screaming at me, waving that buggy whip and sayin' he was a-gonna kill me. I didn't do nothin' wrong, mind you, but that didn't matter to Mr. Alvin. He enjoyed it.

"Somethin' snapped in my head just then," Stuffy continued, pausing momentarily to sneeze. "I turned around and buried that ax in his miserable skull. And right before he croaked, he had the gall to say 'But I'm your grandfather.' And I said 'In a pig's ass you are.' "

"How touching," Fendall said, and got up to make coffee, which was mostly chicory and a smattering of week-old grounds.

While he busied himself, Stuffy reached under the cot and pulled out a white-tipped wooden match, struck against the wall, and set his cot on fire.

"Hey, Mr. Fendall," Stuffy shouted. "Fire in the hole!"

"What in the hell!" Fendall said, having no time to think. He grabbed the water bucket, unlocked the cell, and emptied the bucket on the cot, which was burning six ways from Sunday. One bucket wasn't going to do it, so he handed it to Stuffy and said, "Get me more water!"

Instead, Stuffy bashed the bucket over Fendall's head, leaving a dent in both the bucket and Fendall's skull.

Stuffy ran, his destination anywhere but this crazy town. He ducked into the first house he saw, burst through the door — there was something vaguely familiar about the place — and ran into the downstairs bedroom. He stopped short when it dawned on him whose house he had just invaded.

Hortense Primm was sitting up in bed, aiming her 1820 U.S. military flintlock right at him.

"Oh no," he muttered.

"Oh yes," Miss Hortense said, and fired. The bullet exploded out of the barrel, taking off Stuffy's left ear this time.

"Come back to try again, did ye?" she cried. "Well, this old lady was born pure of body and is sure as hell gonna die pure of body!"

She fired again but Stuffy was already gone. The bullet struck the water pitcher atop the chest of drawers. The pitcher exploded in a shower of hunks of glass.

"Take that, Black Ear Cicero, damn whippersnapper," Miss Hortense growled.

The smoking rocks had started raining down on Sourwood that afternoon.

There were some larger ones, these the size of ripe pumpkins. One smashed into the roof of the livery stable, another hit the roof of the Saddle Sore saloon. Still another went through the roof of Dunderbeck's butcher shop and landed in a barrel of sauerkraut juice.

Smaller ones, still smoking, peppered the streets, smashing windows and sending the few folks still around fleeing in terror. Rocks falling from the sky was something new to them.

Stuffy, bleeding from his wounded head, was running like a frightened rabbit when a rock hit the ground, bounced off a half buried old spur, and hit him square in the face.

He crumpled to the ground, gliding half in and half out of consciousness. Blood trickled down his face from the gash in his forehead, blinding him. He sat up and wiped the blood out of his eyes and was greeted with four very angry men all pointing shotguns at him. He'd murdered their beloved bartender.

"This just ain't your day, son, is it?" one of them said.

Stuffy sneezed.

"Bless you," said a second man, and all four of them opened up and shot Stuffy into a bloody, dead heap.

Fendall, rubbing his sore skull, walked up to the scene and commented, "Man's got more holes in him than a soiled dove's bedsheet."

"He had it coming," said one of the shooters, Webley Hathaway.

"We was gonna hang him, you know," Fendall said.

"Saved you the trouble then," Hathaway said. "Didn't we?"

Chapter 25

Sneed Hearn and Mossy Enright sat around the fire playing the only card game Sneed understood, Go Fish. Mossy, fortunately, knew the game though not well — the last time he'd played Go Fish he was about eight years old.

Mossy had caught two quail, which became dinner. They'd been holed up in their little camp for days. Supplies were almost gone. Dex McGoon went into town day before yesterday and had yet to reappear. Mossy sort of knew McGoon thought he'd be better off without them. And where the hell was Stuffy?

And of course, there was the ever-present blazing ball of hellfire that would scare the snot out of a Trappist monk.

"When McGoon come back?" Sneed asked as Mossy dealt the seven cards to them each. These four words were the first thing Sneed had uttered in a week.

"Your guess is as good as mine," Mossy said, looking up at the sky. The fiery mass was getting closer still. Mossy said, "That thing really gonna wipe us all out, do you think?"

Sneed grunted.

"Think McGoon ran out on us?"

Sneed grunted again.

"Probably not," Mossy decided. "He'd kill us first. Dex doesn't like what he calls 'loose ends.' "

Sneed responded with a grunt, studying his cards.

"Think he'd really kill us?"

Sneed grunted.

"Yeah, that's what I thought."

"You have kings?" Sneed asked. "If so, I take them."

In fact, Mossy had two, king of spades and king of diamonds. He handed them over to Sneed. Mossy said, "Do you have any sevens?"

Sneed grunted and shook his head. Then he said, "Have jack?"

Mossy handed a card over to Sneed, who slapped down three kings and a pair of jacks.

"House is full," Sneed said. "Kings marry jacks."

"Wait a Tuddy pickin' minute," Mossy

said. "What about the two cards you have left over?"

Sneed tossed them into the fire. "No need," he said. "House full."

"You sap," Mossy said. "We ain't playin' poker, for the love of Mike."

"You snore loser," Sneed said with a grunt.

"No, me big dumbbell for playing with you," Mossy said. "And it's 'sore loser,' not 'snore' loser."

Mossy tossed the cards down and said, "I'm sick and tired of settin' on my rump all day waitin' for McGoon. I say we ride into town and raise a little hell."

"Raise hell," Sneed said, and darned if he didn't smile — for the first time in about twenty years — at the thought of slaughtering strangers. And, just maybe, finding a woman, too, with a face a body could look at without shuddering.

"Let's saddle up," Mossy said. He wasn't particularly fond of Sneed Hearn but, like green apple bellyaches and trench mouth, he tolerated him.

Sneed grunted in agreement and off they rode to Sourwood, either to find trouble or make some of their own.

CHAPTER 26

"See that ball in the sky?" Jedadiah Starkwell asked.

"Yes, we've met," Bailey asked, pointing to the comet, which was yet even closer now. "You mean the one that's gonna turn Sourwood into the biggest big fish fry in the history of Texas?"

They were on the porch of the Starkwell ranch. Bailey was standing, looking at the big hunk of misery in the sky. Starkwell was in his wheelchair. It was dusk. The Starkwell boys, Beau and Virgil, were off trying to find any cattle who may have wandered off from the herd. Like everyone else in town, the Starkwells were low on grub.

"Yes, that would be the one," Starkwell said. "Been doing more studying on our situation."

"Why?" Bailey asked, trying to throw off the shroud of hopelessness that tried to settle on him every waking moment. "We're all gonna be dead in what, three days? Four?"

"That's just it," Starkwell said. "I ain't so sure we *are* gonna die."

"What, the comet changed its mind?"

Bailey wasn't in the mood to palaver more about Sourwood's unwanted guest. For one thing, it was getting even closer. For another, most of the folks in town who hadn't run away were losing their mental marbles. Beatings, lynchings, even out and out murder fell over Sourwood like a shroud.

Just this morning, Horace Tidley started chopping firewood like a man possessed and didn't stop until he'd hacked his wife, Mabel Louise, into bloody pieces.

"That'll keep her quiet," Tidley was quoted as saying.

Not an hour later, Ransom Stuckey and Falvey Everhart, normally the best of friends, got into a heated argument about who really won the 1862 Battle of Pea Ridge in Arkansas. Stuckey and Everhart settled the dispute with bullets. When the smoke cleared, they were both dead.

Wolfgang Dunderbeck, wielding a meat cleaver, chased his lady friend Rebeckah Dinwiddie all over town, convinced she was a cooked pork schnitzel and her rear end were twin potato dumplings. It took four men to tackle him and hold him down but not before he bloodied all of them. He was currently locked up in the smokehouse behind his store.

Russell Bunn knocked out his meddlesome brother-in-law, Rufus Dollarhyde, and staked him to an anthill. The fiery Texas ants devoured him up to the knees, prompting Russell Bunn to comment, "He ain't half the man he used to be."

As bodies piled up like cordwood, Doc Cutwater was running out of places to plant them. Agnes Jean and Miss Amelia pitched in to help but it was like dabbing a hemorrhage with a Tuddy ball. Exhaustion was setting in but the two women kept on working feverishly to treat the many injuries. At the moment, Agnes Jean was tending to Dudley "Dud" Skulky, who'd gotten a chunk of buckshot in the ass from farmer Wiley Quick, who thought Dud was stealing his potatoes.

Agnes Jean had planned to move in to the boarding house until Aunt Tinky told her, "That's where your beloved hangs his hat but go ahead and live there. People will talk, you know."

"What people?" Agnes Jean wanted to know. "There's hardly anyone left in Sourwood."

Agnes Jean had to admit her Aunt Tinky had a point. When Miss Amelia offered to put Agnes Jean up at her place — she didn't have much use for Aunt Tinky either — Agnes Jean readily accepted.

"Listen to this," Jedadiah Starkwell said, holding another dusty, unopened book. "In 1705, some guy in England, Sir J. Lyndhurst-Rutherford, wrote about a comet that was seen all over the country — and they also thought it was the end of days. But clearly, it wasn't."

"That's nice," Bailey said, "but did it get as close as our comet? Hell, another day or two, we'll be able to touch it."

"That's just it," Starkwell said. "We won't be touching any part of it. This J. Lyndhurst-Rutherford believed it was the same comet that had been seen seventy years earlier in Arabia. And seventy years before that the comet was seen over the Won Hung Low region of China."

"Well fine," Bailey said. "But what does this mean for us?"

Starkwell said, "Mr. Lyndhurst-Rutherford believed it was the same comet each time, that it circles around in the heavens and comes close to us every seventy years, then vanishes back to wherever it came from."

"What if the comet decides it's tired of all that flying around and wants to catch a few winks?"

Starkwell had no real answer for that but he soldiered on, saying, "Perhaps the comet is like the male of the spec— they never change."

Bailey wasn't buying it.

"Do you know what gravity is, Billy?" Starkwell asked.

He'd heard the word a few times but had no idea what gravity was. He shook his head.

"It's the stuff that keeps us grounded," Starkwell said. "Ever hear of an apple falling up?"

"Can't say as I have."

"It's like when you eat too much and put on more pounds. The blubber goes down to your belly, not to your head."

"One man's opinion," Bailey said. "Sourwood is riddled with blubberheads."

"I can't argue that," Starkwell agreed.

"What exactly does blubber have to do with anything?" Bailey said. "I'm not sure I understand."

"The stuff they call gravity is what pulls the comet down to where we can see it."

"Where does gravity come from?" Bailey asked.

"I dunno," Starkwell said. "Maybe the Lord gave it to us."

"It all sounds good, Jed," Bailey said, "but all I know is what I can see. And what I'm seeing is the road to hell."

"We mustn't give up hope," Starkwell said.

"With all due respect, Jed, please do some hoping for both of us 'cause I need to get back to town before it rips itself into pieces. I ain't ever seen such."

"Things that bad?"

"Well, let's see," Bailey said. "We may be days away from total death and destruction, half the people in town have lit out, the other half have gone plumb loco from fear and hunger, and Agnes Jean still ain't speaking to me."

"Women," Starkwell said. "Can't live with 'em, can't wring their necks and throw 'em down a well."

"No argument here, Jed."

Chester Sturdley rarely partook of spirits — his tolerance for alcohol was low, and according to his late wife, Muriel, he got potted just looking at a whiskey bottle.

Now though, thanks to the generosity of his new friends, he was three sheets to the wind. The whiskey bottle was empty. Sturdley had consumed most of it.

He said, slurring his words, "I ever tell you boys about the time I was surrounded by a Mescalero Apache war party on the Rio Ruidoso River?"

"No, I don't believe you did," McGoon said. "Please share your tale with us, Chester."

"Was 18 and 54," said Sturdley. "I was with the Second U.S. Cavalry out of Fort Conrad . . . or was it Fort Moody . . . may have been Fort Toody . . . or Fort Muldoon . . ."

"Skip that part, Chester," McGoon said.

Goodrich was getting impatient and whispered to McGoon, "Why don't we take him out back and beat the bejesus out of him till he talks?"

"I like my way better," McGoon said. "Please continue, Chester."

"The Apache, oooh, they was murdering devils. Caught us off guard and slit the throats of every man in the regiment and threw 'em in the river. Then . . ."

"Then what?" Goodrich asked, getting even more impatient.

Sturdley drawled, "Then . . . what?"

"We were hoping you could tell us," McGoon said.

"Oh, the hell with it," Sturdley said drunkenly. "Let's all sing."

Sturdley, in a deep baritone, started singing a popular ditty, "Waltz Me Around Again, Tillie."

McGoon slapped his hand over Sturdley's mouth, shutting him up.

"Tell us about this buried gold, Chester, or I'll be forced to cut you from neck to nuts." To prove his point, McGoon produced a Mossy Oak fourteen-inch Bowie knife and pressed the tip of the blade against Sturdley's throat. Sturdley didn't need any further convincing

"M-M-M-Miss Esmerelda's the only one who knows where it's buried," he stammered. Suddenly, he didn't feel all that drunk anymore.

"Who the hell is Miss Esmerelda?" Goodrich asked.

"Widow woman," Sturdley said. "Dead husband went prospecting and hit the motherlode. They buried it and no one knows where."

"Not even if we ask her nicely?" McGoon asked.

"She won't tell you, no matter what you do to her. Heck, she's something like 93 years old — she may not even remember herself."

"We'll see," McGoon said.

"Where does she live?" Goodrich asked.

"And don't think about lying."

Sturdley was sobering up quickly; he felt the beginnings of a headache. "What do you want the gold for? It ain't like you'll have time to spend it. In case you ain't noticed, we got some mighty nasty stuff comin' our way."

"I'll ask you again," Goodrich said. "Where does she live?"

"Can't tell you," Sturdley said. "Promised Miss Esmerelda I'd keep her secret . . . and I done just that."

"Very admirable," McGoon said.

"Folks been huntin' that gold for years," Sturdley said. "Ain't no one found it, neither. And mark my words, you can roast her over an open fire and she still won't tell you. That woman is tougher than an uncured ham!"

"Maybe so," McGoon said. "But my friend here and I can be very persuasive when need be."

"I won't tell you where she lives," Sturdley said, surprised at his own show of bravery. "Even if —"

McGoon pressed the tip of the knife deeper into Sturdley's neck, drawing blood.

"She got herself a cabin two miles west of here," Sturdley said. "Take the Stinkberry Trail to where it forks, one north and one south. Take the north fork."

"Now that wasn't so hard, was it?" McGoon asked. He turned to Goodrich, saying, "Let's get outta here and take us a ride on the Stinkberry Trail."

"Not so fast," Goodrich said. "When this goober sobers up, he'll be babbling to everyone in town about us."

"Got a point there, pard," McGoon said.

"May I borrow your Bowie knife for a moment? I left mine at the boarding house."

McGoon handed Goodrich the knife. Goodrich plunged it deep into Sturdley's gut. He slid off the chair and plopped down to the floor, his lifeless orbs still registering shock.

Goodrich pulled the knife out of Chester Sturdley's belly and wiped the blood off on the dead man's pants. He handed it back to McGoon.

"You're pretty good with that," McGoon commented.

"Practice makes perfect, I reckon," Goodrich responded.

Mossy Enright and Sneed Hearn galloped hell bent for leather into Sourwood, firing their guns in the air, whooping and hollering kicking up a lot of dust.

That is, until they realized the town was

deserted. They halted the horses and looked up and down Main Street

Sneed Hearn said, "No one home."

"Figured that out, did you?" Mossy was puzzled. This wasn't how it was supposed to play out. The idea was to terrorize the folks out of their wits and reign over the whole town with fear and violence.

"Where everybody go?" Sneed Hearn asked. "Where McGoon? Where Stuffy?"

"Maybe in jail," Mossy suggested. "Hell, I'd toss Stuffy behind the iron just for being Stuffy."

"Stuffy think he big poop," Sneed Hearn agreed.

"Let's drop into the jailhouse," Mossy said.

There was nobody inside except for somc old duffer snoring contentedly on the bunk, the cell door wide open. Even asleep, a 44.-caliber Henry rifle was nestled in the old guy's arms.

"Prisoner with gun?" Sneed Hearn asked.

"Never seen such," Mossy said.

The old guy opened his eyes, and still lying on his back, asked, "Help you boys?"

"Do you always sleep with a rifle?" Mossy asked in return.

"Been nicer to me than any woman I ever

knowed," Fendall said. "What can I do you for?"

"We're looking for a friend," Mossy replied. Sneed Hearn nodded in agreement.

"Who isn't?" Fendall said.

"No, you old tosspot," Mossy said. "We're looking for a fella named Stuffy Grandstaff."

"Stuffy Grandstaff, fella was always sneezin'?"

"That would be him," Mossy said. "Know where he is?"

"I'd say the Devil's givin' him a hotfoot in Hell," Fendall said. "We ventilated him yesterday for killin' a bartender."

"Stuffy dead?" Sneed Hearn asked.

"Never seen deader," Fendall said, sitting up, grabbing his Henry, and pointing it at the two outlaws. "He weren't nothin' but a lily-livered, back-shootin' lowlife outlaw. Iffen he's a friend of yours, that probably means you boys are lily-livered, back-shootin' lowlife outlaws, too."

"No, no," Mossy said. "We're, uh, Pinkerton men."

"That a fact?" Fendall said. "You got any papers sayin' you're the Pinks?"

Sneed Hearn pulled a paper out of his pocket and handed it over to Fendall.

Fendall studied it, then said, "This is a

wanted poster for one Sneed Hearn."

"That me," Sneed said with a tinge of pride.

"It sure is," Fendall said.

Mossy elbowed Sneed in the ribs and said, "You dumb cluck."

"He always go around with his own wanted poster?"

"The man has never been close to a mirror," Mossy said. "Had no idea what he looked like. He keeps the poster on him so he doesn't forget."

"If I had a face like his," Fendall said, "I'd try to forget, too."

"And who might you be?" Mossy asked.

"Fendall Harper, retired Texas Ranger and now a deputy here in Sourwood. And I'd say you boys are under arrest."

Mossy and Sneed Hearn both went for their pistols. Fendall fired the Henry twice, one bullet knocking Mossy's hat clean off, the other going between Sneed Hearn's legs, an inch or two below his crotch. They both froze.

"Arrest us for what?" Mossy

"Unless I been livin' in a cave, you boys are part of Dexter McGoon's band of cutthroats. So hands on the back of your miserable heads and no funny business, else I'll put the blast on you both."

Fendall stood, still aiming the Henry at the outlaws, and said, "Into the jug, gentlemen."

"They hang me?" Sneed Hearn asked Mossy.

"I sure as hell hope so. And mind your manners, you no-good tally whackers, else I'll let Wolfie Dunderbeck out of the smokehouse to eat you both," Fendall promised.

There was a pause, then Sneed Hearn asked, "What is tally whacker?"

CHAPTER 27

McGoon and Goodrich dismounted in front of Miss Esme's cabin.

"What an ash heap," Goodrich said. "People actually live in this shack?"

"So sayeth the late Mr. Sturdley," McGoon replied.

The wooden door was pretty solid. McGoon gave the door three swift kicks, forcing it open. They stepped inside.

Inside, Lupita sat at the kitchen table and dabbed at her teary eyes with a dishrag, sniffling.

She said to the strangers, "The door, she was unlocked."

"Miss Esmerelda," Goodrich said. "Is she here?"

"Looking for the gold, *si*?"

"Si, senora," McGoon said. "We'd like to talk with her,"

Lupita said, "You can talk, but Miss Esmerelda not listen."

"We can be very persuasive," Goodrich said.

Lupita shrugged and pointed to the bed. "She right there, but do not expect answer."

They looked over to the bed — there was a lump covered with a sheet.

"That her?" McGoon asked.

"*Was* her," Lupita said. "Miss Esmerelda go to Jesus early this morning."

"In other words . . . she's dead?" Goodrich asked.

"Not in other words," Lupita said. "Yours are good."

Goodrich yanked the sheet off the form on the bed. Sure enough, there was the late Miss Esme. Hands folded across her chest in peaceful repose.

"Damn it all," Goodrich said, and started knocking tearing the place apart.

"Father Dorita come from my village soon, give Miss Esme last rites."

"Don't suppose she told you were the gold is buried?" McGoon axed.

"If she tell me," Lupita said, "I be out now digging it up, and no sitting here with you *higos de putas.*"

"If you *did* know where the gold is buried," McGoon said, "and led us to it, we'd happily share it with you."

"Si," Lupita said. "And then you cut my

throat, take it all. I know not where *oro* is. Miss Esme take her secret to the grave. So *oro* stay where it is. Even if you find, no time to spend it — we all be dead soon."

Neither man saw the point of going on. They turned, left the cabin, and mounted up. They trotted off.

Inside the cabin, Miss Esme sat up and asked, "Are they gone?"

"Si," Lupita said. "And no happy, either. You make very pretty dead lady, Miss Esme. Very good plan, but how you know they coming? You have, what you say, a vision?"

Miss Esme nodded, saying, "They'll be back, Lupita. The greed of men knows no bounds."

Lupita wasn't sure what that meant but she got the idea.

When Bailey returned to the jailhouse, Fendall was dragged a wooden crate filled with wanted posters going back a decade. Bailey eyeballed the two prisoners, who were both dozing, and said, "Got yourself some company, Fendall?"

"Yes indeedy," Fendall said. "I know who the big feller is, but not the little feller, and he ain't talking."

Fendall grabbed a bunch of wanted posters.

"Froggy Gurka," he read. "Bank robbery . . . Sven Stroopwaffel, murder . . . Elmer McBeebee, bank robbery *and* murder . . . Thomas Tewey Bean, also known as Cactus Cal, murder . . . Noodle Ned Nelson, train robbery . . . I remember Noodle Ned, the big lummox. Rangers caught up with him outside a bank in Waco, clobbered him with lead. Orville 'Schnitthead' Schnittberger, killed a U.S. marshal in Oklahoma Territory . . ."

"Any reason why you're looking at old wanted posters?" Bailey asked.

"Big one is Sneed Hearn," Fendall said. "Smaller feller's takin' a vow of silence. Which means he's hidin' something. Dollars to donuts his wretched ass is gracing a wanted poster."

Fendall continued. "Dud Kissel, kidnapping and —" he said in a whisper — "rape."

Fendall whipped through another stack of posters until one in particular caught his eye.

"Well, well, well," he said. "Lookie what I just found."

Bailey looked. There was his silent prisoner. The wanted poster was three years old and the face on it looked younger, but it was him all right, in the flesh.

"I knew it," Fendall said.

"Homer 'Mossy' Enright," Bailey read. "Murder, stagecoach robbery, bank robbery, and —" Bailey blinked his eyes a few times to make sure he was seeing it right — "marrying his horse."

"That one may take some explainin'," Fendall said.

Bailey entered the cell and nudged Mossy awake, clenching the wanted poster. Mossy yawned.

"Did you really marry your horse?" Bailey asked.

Mossy glanced at the wanted poster in Bailey's fist and said, "Course not! What kind of a pre-vert do y'all think I am?"

"You must admit it does sound a little unusual," Bailey said.

"Big joke from Dex McGoon," Mossy said. "We wuz all snockered on moonshine when —"

"You marry horse?" Sneed Hearn asked, awake now. And damn if he wasn't smiling.

"Don't be gettin' no crazy ideas, Hearn," Fendall said.

"Did you say Dex McGoon?" Bailey asked.

"Darn straight," Mossy said. "And when he finds out you got us in here, he's gonna fill you both with a mountain of lead."

"I'm sure he'd be delighted to do just

that," Bailey said. "Until such a time, though, you boys could save yourselves a hanging if you tell me where McGoon is."

"Hell," Mossy said, "hangin' can't be any worse than gettin' all fried up like bacon dancin' on a hot skillet."

"Talkin' to this riffraff is useless," Fendall said. "Now if I was doin' the askin', they'd do the answering, you betcha."

Before Bailey could think on it more, Agnes Jean burst into the jail, out of breath and all aflutter.

"Aggie," Bailey said. "What the —"

"Chester Sturdley's been murdered," she said.

They all looked at Mossy and Sneed Hearn.

"Weren't us," Mossy said. "Tell 'em, Hearn."

"It not us," Hearn replied.

Bailey took Agnes Jean by the arm and led her out the door. He said to her, "How?"

"A very large knife into a very large belly," she said.

"Let's get to it," he said.

"Want me to come?" Fendall asked.

"No," Bailey said, motioning to the two prisoners. "Stay here and do what you got to do."

"The pleasure will be all mine," Fendall

said, and brandished his own knife. "All mine."

Mossy Enright's face went whiter than goat's milk.

Doc Cutwater was already on the scene when Baily and Agnes Jean got there. Chester Sturdley lay very dead on the floor, already attracting horseflies. His blood was everywhere.

"Good Lord," Bailey said. "How long's he been dead, Doc?"

"Three hours, maybe four," Doc said. "One thing's for sure — poor Chester here ain't getting any fresher."

The mercantile smelled like a slaughterhouse. "We best get him planted," Bailey said. "Soon."

Agnes Jean was crying softly. She said, between sobs, "Who'd kill Chester? The man couldn't slap away a bumblebee without feeling bad about it."

"He wasn't just killed," Doc said. "He was butchered."

"You think . . . Wolfie Dunderbeck?" Agnes Jean asked.

"Not hardly," Bailey said. "We got Wolfie locked up in the smokehouse."

"Maybe he escaped," Agnes Jean suggested.

"So he busts out, kills Chester Sturdley, then goes *back* to the smokehouse?" Bailey said.

"Fine, maybe not," Agnes Jean said. "Then who?"

"First Tubby Nooner, now poor Chester Sturdley," Doc said. "What in blazes is going on in this town?"

"Same thing that's likely going on in every town in the territory," Bailey said. "The closer that comet gets, the closer the rule of law goes out the window."

"Then what's the answer?" Doc asked. "Who would do such a thing?"

"Fendall just might have the answer soon," Bailey said.

Agnes Jean said, suddenly remembering, "Mr. Sturdley had some gold nuggets Miss Esmerelda gave him to settle her bill every month. They're gone."

"Take off your left boot and sock," Fendall said to Mossy.

"What fer?" Mossy asked. "You gonna tickle me to death?"

"Just do it," Fendall said.

This old coot meant business. Slowly, Mossy started pulling off his right boot.

"Your *left* boot, featherbrain," Fendall said.

Sneed Hearn giggled. "Man don't know his right from his wrong."

Fendall said, "Pipe down, sidewinder. You're next. And you ain't gonna find anything funny about it."

Mossy pulled off his left boot. His sock was more hole than Tuddy. He yanked it off.

Fendall grabbed Mossy's bare left foot and started slicing into the soft flesh around the ball, making a half-inch cut that squirted blood.

Mossy howled. Fendall asked, "Where's McGoon?"

"In your eye," Mossy said.

Fendall cut deeper into Mossy's foot. Mossy howled even louder.

"I keep cuttin' but you ain't bleedin' enough," Fendall said. "So I'll ask again — where's McGoon?"

Sneed Hearn watched with some degree of horror. He thought he knew everything about torture, but carving a man's foot was something new.

"Eat dirt and die, you old —"

Fendall cut deeper. More blood seeped out of Mossy's foot. He tried to pull his leg away but Fendall had his ankle in a vise-like grip.

"You got some guts, I'll give you that,"

Fendall said, and went to carving Mossy's foot like a Thanksgiving turkey.

"You rotten gut-bucket," Mossy said, whimpering now. "I'll be walking with a limp like an old fart."

Fendall ignored the blood from Mossy's foot leaking all over the jail cell and on his britches. He said, "Limpin' is gonna be the least of your problems if you don't fess up."

To make his point, he cut even deeper into Mossy's foot, saying, "Your little toesies go next."

Mossy looked like he was going to pass out from the pain. Fendall said to Sneed Hearn, "Do me favor and slap your pal a few times."

Hearn didn't need to be asked a second time. He slapped Mossy hard across the face. Mossy revived momentarily then began drifting off.

"Again," Fendall said. "And put a little heat under it this time."

Hearn hauled off and struck Mossy's face hard, almost knocking him off the bunk. It did the trick — Mossy was conscious now. Fendall made like he was going to keep cutting, then Mossy said, "I don't know where he is . . ."

"I'm listenin'," Fendall said, "but I ain't hearing nothing."

Mossy said, "We came to town searchin' for him but he weren't anywhere we looked."

Fendall said to Hearn, "He tellin' the truth?"

Hearn nodded, genuinely afraid now, maybe for the first time in his existence.

Fendall cut Mossy's foot even deeper this time. "Something to remember me by," he said, then pushed the bloody leg away. He'd gotten all he was going to get out of the man.

Mossy's eyes rolled up into his skull until only the whites showed, then passed out colder than a mackerel.

Bailey came back, took one look at his blood-splattered jail. He said,"I'm almost afraid to ask, but what the heck did you do to him?"

"Oh, just a little slicing," he said. "Was about to take an inch or two off his shoe size."

"Get anything out of him?"

"Plenty," Fendall said, "but none that'll do us much good."

Chapter 28

Dex McGoon was holed up in a lean-to a few miles out of town. From the look of things, it had been recently abandoned by its occupants. Couple of down-on-their luck cowboys from one of the ranches in the territory.

The Reverend Thornton Goodrich was on his way back to Sourwood. Before he rode away, he told Dex McGoon, "Someone in that cracker town must know where the gold is buried, and I think I might know just who."

"You wouldn't be thinkin' about digging it up your ownself and cuttin' me out, would you? Cause I wouldn't appreciate that."

"Perish the thought," Goodrich said.

"I've killed more than a few peckerwoods who tried to double-cross me."

"Is that a threat, Mr. McGoon?"

McGoon said, "No, it's a promise."

"All thieves fall out sooner or later, I reckon," Goodrich said.

"For your sake, you best hope it's later."

"Bear this in mind, Dexter," Goodrich said. "Your pretty face is decorating wanted posters from Missouri to Arizona Territory, whereas mine is not. Show yourself in Sourwood and you'll be dancing at the end of a rope before you can slap a tick."

"Maybe," McGoon conceded.

Goodrich said, "I can walk freely in town — far as those jaspers know, I'm a man of God, here to spread the gospel of our Lord."

"What about me?"

"You're needed here," Goodrich said. "I just might not be comin' back alone."

McGoon was confused, followed by angry. "Okay, Goodrich," he said. "Just don't crap in my hat and tell me it fits better."

"Like I said, someone is keeping the location of that gold a secret and I'm reasonably sure I know who it is."

"Not that plumb loco old lady," McGoon said. "She could bite a broomstick in half. Hell, if we cut her fingers and toes off one at a time, she still wouldn't tell us."

"I quite agree," Goodrich said. "But hers isn't the only road open to us."

"Explain to me again, *Reverend,*" Mc-

Goon said, gazing at the massive intruder in the sky, "why are we chasing gold when the whole world is gonna explode in what, two days, maybe three?"

"Perhaps, perhaps not," Goodrich said, "But do you got anything better to do?"

In fact, he did.

Chapter 29

Bailey's Comet, as it was now being called, sported a long blue-white tail as it approached. More chunks of rock fell on Sourwood and vicinity, bigger than before. One piece slammed into the roof of the Saddle Sore Saloon, followed by a fiery explosion that burned the place to the ground and rattled windows from one end of town to the other.

Many comets, asteroids, and meteors haven't changed much in the billions of years since they first formed. Their relatively pristine state can reveal secrets about our origins, chronicling the events that led to the birth of our world, providing clues about the origins of water and minerals that made life possible on Earth — and playing a very large part in the evolution of our planet.

In the distant past, people were both awed and terrified by comets when appeared in the sky unannounced. Chinese astronomers kept extensive records for centuries. The theory is, comets were created during the dawn of our solar system around 4.6 billion years ago.

All of this, of course, was unknown to the folks who stayed behind in Sourwood. Nor would they be even remotely capable of wrapping their minds around it.

The gunshots and screams and bloodshed had ceased. An uneasy silence now lay over Sourwood like a shroud.

Seeing was believing, though, and the general consensus was biblical in nature — the Good Lord was punishing the human race for its sin and immorality and wickedness.

"Seems like the Almighty ain't too happy with the way His creation turned out, and wants to start all over again from scratch," said Miss Flora Mae Fleagle who, with her husband Phineas, owned a small chicken ranch that was now chickenless.

Phineas and Flora Mae Fleagle, along with a dozen or so others, had decided to seek sanctuary in Sourwood's only church, the Sourwood Meeting House. Their greatest fears — and their prayers — were growing in intensity.

"Prayin' ain't no use," said Phineas Fleagle. "When it comes to the Lord, sometimes there ain't no gettin' on His good side when He got somethin' up his snoot."

"Hush, Phineas," Flora Mae said, giving him a solid elbow in the ribs.

"Where's that Reverend Goodrich anyway?" asked Stoddard Ormley, the town street cleaner. Mostly, he cleaned up horse droppings on Main Street. He liked to say, "Their manure is my bread and butter."

"Maybe he lit out, too," Phineas Fleagle said. "The gutless wonder."

"Oh ye of little faith," Goodrich said at the back of the meeting hall. He'd slipped in quietly and unseen.

The burning rocks falling from the sky had ceased almost as suddenly as they had commenced.

Fendall said, "Maybe the Lord ran out."

"I seriously doubt that," Bailey said.

"Makes sense to me," Mossy Enright said, nursing his foot. Doc Cutwater had come by the day before to bandage it up and give Mossy some laudanum to ease the pain. Sneed Hearn hadn't spoken two words since Mossy's ordeal except for, "Hungry. Me."

Bailey had replied, "Sorry, but the kitchen's closed for the foreseeable future. Ain't a tater or a piece of salt pork to be had anywhere."

Fendall said to Hearn, "We're days, mebbe hours from doomsday and you want vittles?"

"I do what belly tell me," Hearn said.

"Then tell your belly to shut its big pie hole," Fendall said.

"Don't say pie," Mossy said. He was hungry, too.

They were sitting in the sheriff's office. Bailey knew he should have been out upholding the law but there wasn't all that much to uphold. Those who remained seemed resigned to their fate, some atoning for their sins, others regretting that they had no real sins to atone for.

The comet was almost upon them or so it appeared. As dusk settled in, the territory was treated to the awe-inspiring spectacle of what looked like a million shooting stars lighting up the sky, like fireworks on the Fourth of July.

"That old sawbones leave me any of that pain medicine?" Mossy asked, his eye glassy. Laudanum and its opium were something new to him. He felt like his brain was spinning in its skull.

Bailey shook his head. "I suspect he's saving it for those who might need it pretty soon."

"Too bad," Mossy said. "A feller could learn to like the stuff."

That same afternoon, the jailhouse door opened and in walked maybe the last person Bailey expected to see: The Comanche war chief, Standing Water. Trailing him was his second in command, Smells the Wind.

Formidable figures both.

An uneasy peace had kept the Comanche and the people of Sourwood from each other's throats for almost a year now. Except for a few cross border raids, where Standing Water and his braves rustled a few heads of cattle or a couple of horses, things were relatively calm.

And Comanche they were, clad in breechcloths and leggings made from soft, tanned deer hides, paired with leather leggings for protection. Both Standing Water and Smells the Wind were adorned with beaded, feathered war bonnets, symbols of courage. These headdresses were decorated with eagle feathers and other ornaments that looked suspiciously like they'd come from the notions department of the mercantile.

"What are them filthy redskins doing here?" Mossy said from the jail cell. "Ventilate 'em!"

"Shut your trap," Bailey said.

Fendall grabbed his rifle and aimed right

at Standing Water's head — he had no love for the Comanche, knowing what tortures of the damned they were capable of. To his credit or fearlessness, Standing Water didn't so much as blink.

Bailey said, "No, Fendall." The Comanche rarely if ever showed themselves in town. The memories of bloodshed between the Comanche and settlers still rubbed raw. Bailey understood this but his job as a lawman was to keep the peace from exploding into another orgy of violence. He treated the warrior tribe with respect, if not trust.

Fendall lowered his gun but only a little.

"Greetings, Standing Water," Bailey said. "Greetings, Smells the Wind."

Standing Water said, in decent English, "We call him Smelly. For small."

"For small?" Fendall asked.

"He means 'for short,' " Bailey said. To Standing Water he asked, though he had a pretty good idea, "What brings you to Sourwood, Standing Water?"

"The spirits are much angry," he said, pointing to the sky. "My people very much afraid."

Smells the Wind added, "Today a good day to die maybe, but Comanche hoping death not in big hurry, wait many more moons."

"Yeah," Fendall said. "I'd say the spirits are in a very bad humor."

"It's what's called a comet," Bailey said.

"Coo-met," Standing Water said. "What coo-met?"

"A big rock coming to us from the heavens," Bailey said. "A gift from God."

"Comanche no need white man's God," Standing Water said.

"Comanche have plenty problem with own god," Smells the Wind added. "Not need more problem from yours."

"What Standing Water tell his people?" the chief asked. "Wisdom of elders fail us."

"They know as much as we do," Bailey said. "Which is very little."

"Elders say we fight this . . . coo-met," Standing Water said. "We kill coo-met."

"Kill coo-met?" Bailey sighed. "Fifteen braves will wage war on a rock that looks as big as Texas?"

Standing Water said, "We rely very heavily on element of surprise."

"There's nothing you or anyone else can do," Bailey said."

"Don't go looking for trouble," Fendall said. "For most folks, it's already there when they wake up in the morning."

"Gather up your tribe," Bailey said, "and get as far away from here as you can."

Standing Water nodded and turned to leave. He said, "Comanche stay and fight."

"Ain't no war dance gonna save your hides this time," Fendall said.

"This is an act of nature," Bailey said. "There's no fighting it."

"Standing Water no agree," the chief said, pounding his chest. "Comanche destroy coomet."

Smells the Wind said to Standing Water, *"Urk looana numu tumak."*

"Smells the Wind say, 'Is better to have less thunder in mouth and more lightning in hand.' "

"Old Comanche proverb?" Bailey asked.

"No," Standing Wolf said. "Smelly read it in *Bazaar Harper.*"

"It's not too late to find a safe place," Bailey said. "Or safer from here, anyway."

Standing Water said, "Dust that thou art from, unto dust thou shalt return."

He walked out, followed by Smells the Wind.

"He's darn loco," Fendall said, "but never met a Comanche who weren't."

"He's entitled to try," Bailey said.

He watched them disappear into the gloom, making sure nobody blew them off their saddles. When it came to the Comanche, folks got itchy trigger fingers. Old habits.

CHAPTER 30

As if Bailey didn't have enough headaches, at sundown the door to the jailhouse blew open in a shower of splinters.

Standing in the entrance, wielding a sawed-off shotgun, was Dex McGoon. Also toting a shotgun was Sneed Hearn. He looked, Bailey noted in that split second, almost giddy with joy. He absolutely adored shooting at things.

"You so much as sneeze and I'll blast y'all," McGoon promised.

Bailey knew better than to draw his gun — he'd never stand a chance. Fendall knew likewise.

"Dex!" Mossy cried. "Never thought I'd be happy to see you."

"What do you want, Mr. McGoon?" Bailey asked.

"What do you think, lawman? I want my boys. Put your guns on the floor and kick 'em over to me."

Bailey and Fendall did just that. Bailey thought for a fast minute about giving the outlaw the keys to the jail cell — what difference did it really make now? They were all going to meet their maker soon enough.

His sense of duty though — and his pride, he had to admit to himself — would not let him surrender his prisoners. But for the moment, he was as good as hog-tied.

"Speakin' of sneezin'," McGoon asked. "Where in blazes is Stuffy?"

"As dead as you're gonna be," Fendall said. "And right quick."

McGoon said, "What the hell are you tryin' to say, you old geezer?"

"He's right, Dex," Mossy said. "Stuffy was kilt by the good folks of this town for shootin' the owner of the saloon."

"Always knew that boy wasn't wrapped too tight," McGoon said.

To Bailey he said, "Toss the old mossback them keys."

Bailey grabbed the keys from the top desk drawer. He tossed them to Fendall but his aim was a little off. They clunked to the floor.

Fendall picked them up, saying, "Old mossback . . . I'm gonna do a barn dance on your stinkin' grave."

"Now let 'em out," McGoon snapped.

Bailey nodded. Fendall unlocked the cell door. Mossy and Hearn darted out, Mossy noticeably limping. He picked up Bailey's pistol.

"Ain't you gonna kill em'?" Mossy asked. "After what they did to me?"

"You got a gun," McGoon said. "Kill 'em your ownself." He and Hearn made a hasty exit.

Mossy shrugged and shot Fendall in the leg, right above the knee. Fendall collapsed into a heap. Bailey's gut reaction was to grab his Colt revolver from the bottom drawer of his desk but Mossy spun around and aimed at him point blank. One shot and most of Bailey's face would disappear.

"Whatever you're thinkin', don't," Mossy said. "This don't come close to payin' you back, you old toad, but I'll be a-comin' back to finish the job."

"You best be on your way," Bailey said. " 'Cause if it takes me the rest of my life, I'ma hunt you down like the mad dog you are."

"Yeah, you and the U.S. Cavalry," Mossy said, and fired a shot in Bailey's direction. Billy dived for cover as the bullet slammed into the wall.

"Will you get your useless butt out here, now!" McGoon shouted from outside.

"This ain't over," Mossy said, and limped out into freedom.

Bailey shouted to Fendall, "Quick — run out and get Doc Cutwater."

"In case you ain't noticed, Billy," Fendall said, his leg bleeding pretty good now, "my runnin' days just come to an end."

Bailey scrambled to his feet and yanked the Colt from his desk. By the time he cleared the door, however, the terrible trio had mounted up — McGoon had stolen the few remaining horses that hadn't been eaten by the starving residents of Sourwood. From an abandoned ranch outside of town, no less.

"Lousy rat left his horses to die," McGoon had commented to himself.

Bailey fired a couple of shots at the fleeing trio, galloping hell for leather into the distance and out of range.

Doc Cutwater, with Agnes Jean's help, patched up Fendall as best he could, removing the bullet and cauterizing the wound. Bailey had slung Fendall over his shoulder and carried him over to Doc's office.

Fendall had passed out. Doc said, "He's lost a lot of blood, Billy."

"Is he going to make it?" Bailey asked.

"If it was anyone else," Doc said, "I'd say

probably not, but Fendall is a tough old bird."

"What can we do?" Agnes Jean asked.

"No," Doc said. "You might as well go on home and hope for the best, both of you. We'll have a better idea come morning. That is, if any one of us are still alive and kicking."

"Mind if I walk with you?" Bailey asked Agnes Jean.

"I can't very well stop you," she said.

They strolled silently for a spell. Agnes Jean had moved back to her Aunt Tinky's house. She didn't seem too happy about it. Aunt Tinky was as stubborn as a horse trader's mule, not to mention mean-spirited, but in all fairness, she refused to flee like so many others in town had.

"Are you still angry with me?" Bailey asked.

"You have no idea," she replied.

"What are you thinking?"

"I'm thinking maybe Aunt Tinky was right about you," she said.

Bailey's blood was simmering and was about to boil over. He said, "And maybe you should marry Royal Briggs instead!"

"Maybe I will," she responded. "It will free you up to marry Matilda Mae Dinsmore. Everyone knows you always had an eye for her."

"An eye," Bailey said. "Not my heart."

"Oh, pish posh," she said. "I could always marry Rufus Flannery."

"Go ahead," Bailey said. "Flannery will get you nowhere."

"He's not an unreasonable, hard-nosed, pimple-headed, stiff-necked, single-minded, square-toed, cantankerous scoundrel like some people it's been my misfortune to know!"

"Am I really all of those things?" Bailey asked.

"All of them and more," she said.

"Would you at least tell me why you're angry with me?"

"You don't remember?"

"To be perfectly honest," Bailey said, "no."

"Well, to begin with, you could have —"

"Quit jabbering," he said, and took Agnes Jean into his arms. He kissed her deeply and with more passion than he ever thought possible. Agnes Jean wrapped her arms around him in return and kissed him back just as passionately.

Bailey loved the feel of her voluptuous body and the swell of her breasts against his.

Damn, did he love her.

"Now," he said, "you were saying?"

"Shut up and kiss me again, stupid."

"Your wish is my every command," he said, and kissed her again, embracing her even more tightly if that was possible.

"Are we really going to die, Billy?" She stifled a sob. "I'm so frightened."

"Not today," he said. "And not tomorrow or the day after tomorrow. I won't let that happen, not ever."

She said, "You know, I could get to like you," she said.

"I can't bear the thought of not being with you till hell freezes over," he said. "Maybe we should light out like most of the others have."

"Not on your kidney plaster," Agnes Jean said. "Without this town, you'd die! Sourwood is the only home you've ever known, it's part of you, in your blood. And you'll never leave till you're carried out in a pine box."

"I'll say it again, Agnes Jean. I'm nutty as a fruitcake for you."

"You do know how to charm a lady," she said.

Bailey held her close and felt an inconvenient stirring below the waist. He thought Agnes Jean would push him away but she held him even closer, almost knocking the wind out of him.

She whispered in his ear, "I don't want to die before I've . . . before we've . . . I don't want to die . . . unloved."

Bailey wasn't sure he was hearing her correctly but he wasn't fool enough to ask. Instead, he said, "Then let's get married — now, tonight."

"It doesn't matter if we're married or not, Billy," she said. "It's time to . . . get biblical."

"It matters to me," Bailey said.

"But there's no one to marry us," Agnes Jean said. "No judge, no minister . . ."

"You forget, Aggie," Bailey said. "I'm also a justice of the peace in my role as deputy marshal."

"I'm not sure I understand," she said. "You mean you can marry us yourself?"

"I believe so," he said. "I do, though, legally, have to appoint myself."

"How?"

Bailey raised up his right hand, pressed his left against his badge. He said, "I, Deputy Marshal William Thaddeus Bailey of Sourwood, Texas, hereby appoint William Thaddeus Bailey justice of the peace."

"Is that legal?" Agnes Jean asked,

"It'll do," he said.

As they sealed the deal with another passionate kiss, a fiery hunk of comet the size of a baby elephant crashed into Lomax Milligan's barbershop and exploded on impact, illuminating half the town.

"I'd say Milligan got that deep hole he wanted," Agnes Jean said.

"Poop on fire and save the matches," he said suddenly. "I forgot!"

"Forgot what?"

"Miss Esmerelda," he said. "McGoon and his gorilla apes are gonna go after her gold, I can feel it." He looked at Agnes Jean. "They'll torture her if they have to."

"Good Lord," Agnes Jean said. "We best get to her, bring her back to town."

"Where is she gonna stay?"

"I think I have an idea," she said. "Get the buckboard."

"Where's Lupita?" Bailey asked.

Miss Esmerelda puffed on her corncob pipe and said, "I sent her home to be with her family when the end times git here. Why ain't you home with your'n?"

"I ain't got one," Bailey said.

"You need to come with us, Miss Esmerelda," Agnes Jean said. "The McGoon gang will be at your door anytime now."

"I sent those prairie rats away last time," the old gal said, "and iffen I ran off ever' time some mush-mouth peckerwood came a-huntin' for my gold, I'd die of shame."

"All good and well, Miss Esmerelda," Bailey said, "but you don't know these devils. They'll torture you!"

"I know all about torture," Miss Esmerelda said. "Don't forget I was married once."

Bailey said to Agnes Jean, "Gather up whatever you think she'll need." To Miss Esmerelda he said, "I'm taking you to town if I have to carry you on my back."

"You ain't carryin' me no place," Miss Esmerelda said. "I'll be sleepin' warm and cozy in my own bed when the end comes, and not before."

Agnes Jean grabbed clothes and packed them up in a big straw basket. She pulled a very old and musty nightgown that was in the late stages of falling to pieces. She held it out to Miss Esmerelda.

"You put that back, you brazen hussy," the old lady snapped.

"It's very pretty," Agnes Jean said.

"Wore it once — on my weddin' night." She snorted. "For all the good it done me."

Agnes Jean let that one pass. She asked, "Do you want to take it?"

"Why?" Miss Esmerelda asked. "I ain't leavin'."

"But you are," Bailey said. He stepped out

onto the porch, grabbed her rocking chair and put it onto the buckboard. He came back for more of her stuff.

"In a pig's eye," Miss Esmerelda screeched. She grabbed a cast iron frying pan from the stove, and in a surprising show of strength, flung it at Bailey as he stepped back inside. He ducked and the pan flew about two feet over his head. Bailey was momentarily impressed — that frying pan looked like it weighed ten pounds at least. The old girl still had plenty of fight in her.

She grabbed whatever she could get her hands on. She threw battered old tins that once held coffee and flour and salt, then wooden utensils, whatever she could get her hands on. Plates. Cups. Saucers. Baily dodged them all. They shattered on the floor.

"You get out of my home, you dad-blasted hooligan!" Miss Esmerelda grabbed the tea kettle and hurled it at him.

Bailey wasn't quite quick enough. The kettle bounced off his head, leaving a little gash. Blood trickled down his forehead.

"Oww!" Bailey shouted, wiping blood away with his sleeve. "Damn, Miss Esmerelda, that hurt."

"Was supposed to, you addle-brained

swamp rat," she said.

She picked up a very long, sharp carving knife, and it seemed, with every intention of ramming it into Bailey's belly. She was surprisingly spry for a woman her age.

"No, Miss Esmerelda!" Agnes Jean yelled.

Bailey grabbed her wrist and gave it a twist. She dropped the carving knife. Bailey released her arm. She punched him squarely on the nose.

"That'll be enough of *that,*" Bailey said. He grabbed her around the waist and threw her over his shoulder. He carried her out to the buckboard and eased her, kicking and screaming, into her rocking chair.

Taking no chances, he tied her to the chair with some old rope she'd used as a clothes-line. She continued screaming, which would have normally sent the flock of black-chinned hummingbirds who nested in a live oak tree near the cabin scattering into the winds. Only the birds, knowing something bad was happening, had flown away a week ago.

Bailey found an old scarf among her clothes. He said, "I am truly sorry to have to do this, Miss Esmerelda."

He stuffed the scarf into Miss Esmerelda's mouth.

Agnes Jean, carrying a basket full of

undergarments, said, "Is that really necessary, Billy?"

"I can't have her screaming bloody murder all the way back to town. It annoys people."

"Where are we taking her?" she asked.

"To Miss Hortense Primm's house," he said. "She's got plenty of room."

"We can't do that, Billy," Agnes Jean said. "Everyone knows Miss Esmerelda and Miss Primm have hated each other for half a century, maybe longer."

"Good," Bailey said. "Maybe they'll do us all a favor and kill each other."

"That's not funny," Agnes Jean said.

"It wasn't meant to be."

He hopped down off the buckboard and said, "I'm gonna fetch Doc Cutwater. Don't do anything till we get back."

Miss Hortense Primm had been looking out the front window to survey the weather. The sky was the unnatural color of mustard that had been left in the sun for a week. There was not even the hint of a breeze. The air seemed thick, like breathing through a wet towel.

It was then that Miss Primm was treated to a very strange and puzzling sight indeed.

A buckboard wagon had stopped directly in front of her house. Though her eyesight wasn't what it had been, she still saw what curiously looked like a person tied up in a rocking chair.

She was having one of her more lucid days. She stepped out onto the veranda for a closer look. Took her a minute or two, but she dimly recognized the lady in the rocker.

"It can't be," she said. "It just can't be."

She watched as Bailey and Agnes Jean struggled to get the rocker off the back of the buckboard.

"Oh, in the name of St. Michael," she said. "You pathetic weaklings." She picked up the rocker effortlessly and handed it off to Bailey, who set it on the ground. "Can you get the chair inside?" he asked Agnes Jean.

"I think I can manage it," she said. Bailey dashed off to Doc Cutwater's office.

"Is that Esmerelda?" Miss Hortense half said, half screamed. "Or do my eyes deceive me?"

"Miss Esmerelda needs a place —" Agnes Jean started.

Miss Esmerelda sat down in her rocking chair, creating an incongruous sight ten yards from Miss Hortense's door. She said, "Damn right, it's me, Hortense Primm," Miss Esmerelda said. "Cain't see ya, but I can sure as hell smell ya. What're you usin' for perfume, sump weed?"

"I can see the years haven't been kind, you cackling old biddy. You're dirty and foulmouthed and an abomination to God! And you still got a face like a bucket of pond scum!"

"Me?" Miss Esmerelda said, "Hell, you're so ugly you gotta sneak up on a glass of water!"

"And are you still the old whore of Babylon?" Miss Hortense retorted. She added, mostly for Agnes Jean's benefit, "Bet you didn't know Esmerelda gave her body to half the men in the territory. She even brought her boyfriend to her husband's funeral!"

"Still claimin' to be as pure as the driven snow, Hortense?"

"Shut your —"

Miss Esmerelda said, "You ain't still peddlin' that banana oil, are you?"

"Well," Agnes Jean started to say. "I think Miss Henri—"

"Why, sweet, innocent, precious little Hortense Primm hit the goose down mattress with half the soldiers in Fort Stockton."

"That's a lie," Miss Hortense said. "And so help me, if you weren't blind I'd rip your hair out one at a time!"

"Even if I was crippled in both legs and still blind in both eyes, I could still whomp your butt to hell and back!"

The insults got heated and turned to out and out screaming.

"Miss Hortense isn't really untouched?" Agnes Jean murmured, mostly to herself.

CHAPTER 31

"You took her where?" Doc Cutwater asked with a touch of astonishment.

He'd been mixing up his own brand of Silk Hat Harry's Magic Humor Cure Elixir — laudanum, wood grain alcohol, oil of wintergreen, camphor, sugar, some cinnamon, and staggering amounts of wood grain alcohol — which he had kept hidden after the Saddle Sore ran out of whiskey.

Doc Cutwater was mixing up a large batch — not for fun or profit, but to dispense to the townsfolk when, or if, the end came. Doc had concocted it so that folks would be happily high during the crack of doom.

To test it, Doc had given a few teaspoons of the stuff to Fendall, who said, "Tastes like a wild hog did his business in it. Smells like it, too." A minute or two later, Fendall was flying higher than Pike's Peak.

Watching Fendall's eyeballs rolling around in his head, Doc was satisfied his home remedy would be effective. He filled two dozen glass bottles with the liquid. Fendall had been quite correct — it smelled like an outhouse in August.

But it worked.

"You took Miss Esmerelda to stay with Hortense Primm? Are you insane? They'll be at each other's throats faster than two farts in a tailwind."

"Yes," Bailey said. "Agnes Jean held the same opinion."

"Then why, Billy?"

"Because McGoon and his cutthroats want her gold, and they'll skin her alive if she doesn't tell them where it's buried."

"What can they do with gold?" Doc asked. "It'll be about as useful to them as feathers on a fish."

"Yes," Bailey said, "can you think of a better place for her to hole up than in the home of her mortal enemy? It's the last place they'll look for her."

"Oh, mule fritters," Doc said. "I wish to the Lord that old crone would just tell them where it's buried so they'll dig it up and hopefully leave Sourwood."

"They'll never get the chance," Bailey said.

"And why is that?

" 'Cause it's my turn to dance on their

miserable graves," Bailey said.

"I believe it was Aristotle who said, 'No happy man can become miserable, for he will never do acts that are hateful and mean.' "

Fendall was half in and half out of consciousness. Still, he said, " 'Lead us not into temptation. Just tell us where it is — we'll find it.' "

"Did Aristotle say that?" Bailey asked.

"No," Fendall said. "I did."

He closed his eyes and was sound asleep in a heartbeat.

Later that afternoon, Doc Cutwater, and Agnes Jean were sitting in Miss Hortense's parlor. She and Miss Esmerelda glared at each other. Well, Miss Hortense glared at her; Miss Esmerelda glared back and hoped she was shooting daggers at the right person. Doc Cutwater was attempting to hold court. Bailey had strapped on his guns and gone hunting for the McGoon gang.

He said, "So this farmer walks into a café and asks the proprietor, 'How do you prepare your chicken?' And the proprietor says, 'We just tell 'em straight out they're gonna die.' "

The joke, an attempt to defuse the tension, as Doc knew it would, fell flatter than a johnnycake.

Miss Hortense said, "I do not want this wanton tramp under my roof!"

"And I'd rather live with a nest of rattlesnakes," Miss Esmerelda said.

"After you," Miss Hortense said, "a rattlesnake would be a step up." She added, "I hope that big rock falls on your stupid head."

"Everyone in town knows you ladies don't particularly care for each other," Doc Cutwater said. "But would one of you kindly explain the root of your mutual animosity?"

"In 1823, Miss Hortense Primm —" Miss Esmerelda started.

"It was 1821," Miss Hortense said. "Not 1823. As you can see —"

Miss Esmerelda: "It *was* 1823, you ignorant —"

Miss Hortense paused, then said, "The Devil's bride, that's what you are! Being a Christian woman —"

Miss Esmerelda: "If I was the Devil's bride, you'd be the maid of honor —"

Miss Hortense: "The root of all evil — that's what —"

"That's enough!" Doc Cutwater shouted, smacking an end table. "Death and destruction and misery are waiting right outside the door and you two old bats are fighting like two weasels in a burlap sack — fighting over something that happened fifty years ago?"

"Fifty-one years ago," Miss Hortense said.

"It was fifty-three years ago," Miss Esmerelda said.

"Fifty-one, you toad in the hole!"

"How can you remember anything? Your brain's about as sharp as rice pudding!"

"At least I have a brain," Miss Hortense said. "Only thinking you ever done was on your back."

"That tears it," Doc Cutwater said. "You two simmer down or my hand to God, I'll kick you both till you're dead."

The two old gals quieted down.

"Now," Doc Cutwater said, pointing to Miss Esmerelda, "I want you, Miss Esme, to tell me in no more than five words why you and Hortense have been feuding for more than half a century."

"That old crow —" she started to say.

"That's three words," Doc Cutwater said. "You got two left."

"Drop dead," Miss Esmerelda said. "That's five."

"Didn't think she could even count that high," Miss Hortense commented.

"Your turn, Hortense," Doc said, and the result was pretty much the same, a barrage of salty curses and insults. Doc was taken aback — he couldn't believe Miss Hortense even knew those dirty words.

"Let me try," Agnes Jean said.

"Be my guest," Doc said.

To Miss Esmerelda and Miss Hortense, she asked, "I'll take a shot in the dark here, and I'm asking you both, was a man involved? They usually are."

Neither of them responded.

"Your silence speaks volumes," Doc said.

"Well of course a man was involved, you dumb dora," Miss Esmerelda said.

"And he was . . . whom?"

"Name of Luther Piffle," Miss Esmerelda said.

"I will not be in any way a part of this . . . madness," Miss Hortense said. "This conversation is downright sacrilege, blasphemy, and a desecration of my dignity, soiling my spirit and casting aspersion on my reputation.

"And his name was Lucius, not Luther!"

"For the first time in her life, she's right," Miss Esmerelda said. Then, as if remembering, "Ah, Luscious Lucius — what a man!"

Agnes Jean asked, curious now, "So what happened?"

"Luscious was a lieutenant under Captain William Carey's artillery company," Miss

Esmerelda said. "Died fightin' at the Alamo back in '36."

"And he couldn't decide which one of you fine ladies he liked better?" Doc asked.

"Poppycock," Miss Esmerelda said. "He was tearin' up the sheets with the both of us! Only we didn't know he was two-timing us. Stinkin' piece of dirt."

"Lies, nothing but lies! Not even sun-up and that filthy mouth is already open for business," Miss Hortense said.

"What's in the past stays in the past," Agnes Jean said, getting a little hot now. "So quit your moaning and groaning and try to act civil. Who knows — in a few days, maybe a week, none of this bat guano you two are flinging all over creation will even matter. So would you both stop arguing and start acting your ages!"

"Tried that once," Miss Esmerelda said. Didn't suit me."

"It wouldn't," Miss Hortense sniffed. "Not if there was even one man around with a stiff —"

"Hortense Primm!" Doc Cutwater said. "Stop that."

"I want you both to swear you'll stop squabbling," Agnes Jean said. "Things are bad enough without your pettifogging."

"I swear," Miss Hortense said, though she

didn't sound too pleased. Agnes Jean turned to Miss Esmerelda. "And do you swear —"

"No," Miss Esmerelda said, "but I know all the words."

"Miss Esmerelda —" Agnes Jean was having none of it.

"Oh, all right," Miss Esmerelda said. "Fetch me my bible — if I got to swear, I'd prefer to do it on the Good Book."

Agnes Jean looked around but didn't see it. She rummaged through the crate filled with Miss Esmerelda's possessions, but it wasn't there either. She said, "I can't quite locate it. Maybe Miss Hortense would let you swear on hers."

"Perish the thought," Miss Hortense said.

"I don't want her smelly bible, I want *mine.* Don't tell me you didn't pack it."

"A bible is a bible," Doc Cutwater said. "What difference does it make?"

"Plenty, you old sawbones," Miss Esmerelda said. "That bible is where I hid the map to the gold."

"What?" Agnes Jean and Doc Cutwater said in unison.

"I figure if a heathen is tryin' to find the map to my gold, last place he'll look is in the bible."

"God give me strength," Doc Cutwater said.

"Never mind God givin' you strength," Miss Esmerelda said. "Ask Him to git me my good book. The map is there, where I put it all them years ago, right between Proverbs and Ecclesiastes."

"I best ride out there and fetch it then," Agnes Jean said.

"That ain't a good idea, Agnes Jean," Doc Cutwater said. "The McGoon gang is holed up somewhere and my guess is, it isn't far."

"Won't take any time at all," Agnes Jean said, and headed out.

"All these years wondering," Doc Cutwater said. "When it was right under our noses."

"I wouldn't say that," Miss Esme said. "Not exactly."

Agnes Jean mounted up. She'd unhitched the horse from the buckboard and trotted out to Miss Esmerelda's cabin.

She couldn't shake the bad feeling in her belly. Maybe this was a fool's errand.

"I'm sure Mr. McGoon and his boys are far, far away by now," she said to herself, not quite believing it. "Of course, if Billy has probably put them in the ground by now."

"Ain't no one home, looks like," Mossy Enright said.

His foot was still throbbing. When all this was over, he aimed to go back to Sourwood and kill that miserable old duffer they called Fendall.

The floor of the cabin was still strewn with the pots and pans and everything else Miss Esmerelda had hurled at Bailey.

"Maybe we ain't the only one lookin' for that gold," Goodrich said.

"Look like big twister rip through here," Sneed Hearn said.

"Maybe she lit out," McGoon said.

"Goodrich said. "Or she wants it to look that way. I bet the gold is stashed someplace."

"Here?" Mossy asked. "In this cabin? I thought it was buried."

"Only one way to find out," McGoon said. "Let's look."

"Check everywhere, under the floorboards, behind the walls, rip this place from top to bottom, up the chimney," Goodrich said. "And try to think like you're an old lady — where would she hide it?"

"Maybe it's under the outhouse," Mossy said, trying to lighten the mood. "I bet the old girl spends a lot of time in there."

"A superb idea, Mr. Enright," Goodrich said. "We'll leave that joyous task in your capable hands."

"They ain't that capable," Mossy grunted. He paused, waiting for Goodrich to tell him it was just a joke, until McGoon said, "You heard him, Mossy. And look inside the crapper. I wanna see your arms covered in waste matter. Now git."

Mossy grunted again, shaking his head. "I got to find me a new bunch to ride with."

The gang set about tearing Miss Esmerelda's cabin to shreds. For good measure, Sneed Hearn ripped the front door off its hinges.

There stood Agnes Jean. Her eyes widened in fear and surprise, looking like two poached eggs. She opened her mouth to scream but her voice wouldn't cooperate.

"Well, well, well," Goodrich said, with a sinister smile. "Look what the cat dragged in."

"Reverend Goodrich?" Agnes Jean said. "What are you doing with these . . . men?"

Dex McGoon was an outlaw and a killer. His gang, Sneed Hearn and Mossy Enright, were almost as bad. Yet it was the Reverend Thornton Goodrich, seemingly the most civilized of this unholy bunch, who frightened her the most. It was his eyes — black, unblinking, devoid of compassion — that spooked her. He was smiling as those lifeless eyes gazed up and down her shapely form, as if making malevolent plans for what he planned to do to her. She shivered at the thought.

McGoon's evil-minded cohorts also stared at her, no doubt making some plans of their own. *Let them,* Goodrich thought. They were welcome to Miss Agnes Jean, but only when he was done with her.

McGoon wasn't as patient. He hauled off and backhanded her, knocking her flat onto the floor.

"Where is it?" he asked.

Agnes Jean dabbed at the blood seeping from her split lower lip. Wiping it away, she said, "I don't know. And if I did, I wouldn't tell you." She looked at Goodrich and said, "I might've known you'd find your fellow degenerates. *Reverend* in a pig's poke."

McGoon kicked her hard. Agnes Jean rolled onto her side, but would not scream or cry for help. They'd kill her, of course, she had no doubt about that.

"Easy, Mr. McGoon," Goodrich said. "This fetching young morsel of womanly charm has more uses than just a punching bag."

"She knows," McGoon said. "I'd bet my boots on it." To Agnes Jean he said, "Tell us or die. Those are your choices."

She said, "Why should I? You're gonna kill me either way. And if you don't, that ball of fire in the sky will, and soon. So why should I?"

"Because, kind, loving soul that Mr. McGoon is," Goodrich said, "he can kill you quick with a bullet to the head. Or else take his sweet time introducing you to the tortures of the damned."

"Yeah, and your coward of a boyfriend ain't ridin' to the rescue neither," Mossy said, trying to show support for his boss.

McGoon and Goodrich glared daggers at him. Mossy tried a weak grin. He said, with a wave of his hand, "I thought we were on the same . . . never mind. You boys are doing fine."

McGoon said, "Get her up."

"Don't cut her up too much," Goodrich said. "Leave some for the rest of us."

Sneed Hearn and Mossy lifted Agnes Jean to her feet and plopped her down into a rickety wooden chair. Mossy rummaged around and found some clothesline. He wrapped it all snug and cozy around her, pinning her arms behind her.

"Now keep looking for that map," McGoon ordered. The gold wasn't anywhere in the cabin, so it had to be buried nearby.

Mossy and Sneed Hearn went back to tearing the cabin apart. That's when Agnes Jean spotted it. A dusty stack of books on the fireplace mantel sat undisturbed. On top was a volume of Walt Whitman poetry but Miss Esmerelda didn't like them because they didn't rhyme.

Underneath was *Silas Marner.* Miss Esmerelda didn't like that one either, because when Lupita read it to her in her heavily accented English, everything sounded Mex.

Underneath *Silas Marner* was Miss Esmerelda's bible. The old gal had been right — Hearn and Mossy had ignored the books.

At one point, Sneed Hearn, growing impatient, angrily swept the three books off the mantel and onto the floor. The bible landed about four feet from where Agnes Jean was strapped down. A little piece of wrinkled piece of paper was visible.

McGoon slapped her again, and growled, "I want that damned map!" He kicked the bible in frustration, where it smacked against a leg on the kitchen table and tumbled open.

The neatly folded piece of paper popped out.

"Well bust my buttons," Goodrich said.

McGoon unfolded it, expecting a map of some kind. He read, "Look in the coffee tin on the top shelf."

The coffee tin was exactly where the note said it would be. Inside was another note.

Goodrich grabbed it away and looked at it. He read, "Drop your britches and eat your socks, look right under that pile of rocks."

"What in blazes does that mean?" Mossy asked.

Goodrich said, "If I didn't know better, I'd say Miss Esmerelda was fond of treasure hunts. What do you think, Miss Agnes Jean?"

"You would have to ask her," she said, "but it does seem to be the case."

McGoon was not happy. He said to his men, "Get out there and look for a pile of rocks, you nitwits."

"There's a million piles of rocks out there," Mossy protested. "How will we know which one?"

They all turned to Agnes Jean, still struggling to squeeze out of the rope.

"Maybe you'd like to answer that question?" Goodrich said to her.

She said, "Listen for the voices of the spirit guides wandering in the winds. They will say 'The gold is here . . . come take the pretty gold.' "

"Okay then," Mossy said to Sneed Hearn.

"Let's go out and wait for the voices."

They started out until McGoon said, "She's yanking your chain, you horse's rump."

Goodrich said, "Let's *all* go out and wait for the voices, shall we?"

There were no voices on the wind but the pile of rocks — the right one — wasn't too hard to find.

Agnes Jean was sitting on a tree stump, watching as the four outlaws flung rocks from the pile. There was nothing underneath except dirt.

Goodrich said, "Dig we must."

A little less than a foot below, a portion of a glass bottle with a cork in it glinted in the sunlight. Goodrich pulled it from the ground. Inside was another piece of paper. He yanked the cork out with his teeth, spit it out and tried to get the paper with his pinkie. When that didn't work, he smashed the bottle with a rock.

He opened the note and read: "Search the deer head, idiot."

They trooped back into the cabin. The deer head was mounted right there — it was hard to miss.

McGoon grabbed a step stool and placed it under the deer head. He was about to step up, then thought better of it and said to Sneed Hearn, "You do it."

Hearn shook his head. "Bad, bad medicine," he said.

"It won't bite," McGoon assured him.

Hearn opened the deer's mouth and gingerly stuck his hand inside. They all heard the crackling of paper. Their breathing quickened.

Hearn opened the note — it was brown with age — and stared at it.

"What the hell does it say?" McGoon asked.

Hearn said, "Don't know."

"He doesn't know how to read," Mossy said.

McGoon grabbed the note and handed it to Mossy. "Then you read it."

"I cain't read neither."

Goodrich impatiently snatched the note from Mossy's hand. He read, "Have you looked inside the butter churn?"

"Butter churn?" McGoon said. "Darn crazy old lady! If I ever get my hands around her scrawny neck . . ."

Despite her pain, not to mention her precarious situation, Agnes Jean giggled.

"What's so damn funny?" McGoon asked.

For some reason, Agnes Jean wasn't afraid anymore. Yes, they were going to kill her —

but she was resigned to her fate.

She said, "Aren't you going to check the butter churn?"

They did. This note read, "Why not try the sewing basket?"

"What sewing basket?" Goodrich asked Agnes Jean.

"Probably the one where she kept her needles and thread."

Goodrich pulled his knife and pressed the tip of the blade under Agnes Jean's nose.

"This is not," he said, "the best time to make me even angrier."

"Here it is," Mossy said, picking through a mountain of household stuff and pulling it out. "Must have been in the chest of drawers we toppled over."

McGoon flipped it open, stuck his hand inside, and yelped like a wounded coyote. Half a dozen sewing needles were sticking out of his palm.

Goodrich snatched the note away.

The note said, "You still ain't found it cause if you had, you wouldn't be reading this."

McGoon angrily let out a string of obscenities that would have made the Barbary pirates blush.

Mossy said, "This is getting monogamous!"

"All right then," Goodrich said to Agnes Jean. "Tell us where she is or so help me, I'm going to cloud up and rain all over you."

"I don't *know* where she is," Agnes Jean said.

"Oh, come now," Goodrich said. "You came here to fetch something of hers — the map maybe?"

"Even if I knew where she was, and even if there *was* a map," Agnes Jean said, "she'd never tell you, me, or anybody. That woman is suspicious of her own nose."

"Let's just kill her and head to town," McGoon said. "We'll find the old crow if she's there."

"And waste this delightfully lovely embodiment of feminine glamour and grace?" Goodrich said.

"What he say?" Sneed Hearn asked Mossy.

"Ain't sure," Mossy said. "I think it means —"

"It means," Goodrich said, "this little lady is our ace in the hole." He turned to Agnes Jean. "It's very simple — your life for that map, or better still, the location of the gold."

"You mean we ain't gonna be able to see her with no britches on?" Sneed Hearn grunted in agreement.

"Business before pleasure," Goodrich

said. "If you're good boys, you'll be given the opportunity to gaze at this lovely creature in the so-to-speak."

"To-so-speak?" Sneed Hearn asked.

"It means *naked,* imbecile," McGoon said.

"Get her on her feet, Mr. McGoon. She's coming with us," Goodrich said.

It was dawning on Dex McGoon that somehow, somewhere along the line, the Reverend Thornton Goodrich had quietly taken control of the McGoon gang, or what was left of it.

Well, he'd settle the good reverend's hash soon enough. And permanently.

CHAPTER 32

Deputy Marshal William Bailey had searched every possible hiding spot in and around the town looking for McGoon and his gang of merry men.

He looked in Buttermilk Creek, a few miles south of Sourwood and a roost popular with outlaws. There was no buttermilk in Buttermilk Creek; in fact, there wasn't even water — it had dried up ages ago.

He then tried Stanky's Mill, a dilapidated structure where once it had turned grain crops into flour. Norval Stanky, who had founded it in 1843, died ten years later. Poor Stanky forgot the combination to the office safe and in frustration gave it a swift kick. The safe didn't open; all Stanky got for his efforts were two broken toes. Which he ignored until his left leg from the knee down swelled up and had to be amputated when gangrene set in.

But it was too late — the gangrene spread

and the rest of the leg had to go. Then his right leg became gangrenous and off it was cut. By this time, there wasn't much of Norval Stanky left to infect but the damage was done. Stanky died shortly thereafter.

McGoon and his boys weren't there, nor had they been from the looks of things.

Bailey's next stop was Clutter's Trading Post, which closed up after Egbert Clutter tried to cheat a couple of Comancheros, who butchered him, cut him into pieces and tossed them into the Guadalupe River. Said one Texas Ranger, "Clutter always wanted to be a man about town but not in different pieces."

The place was abandoned and had been in various stages of crumbling ever since.

McGoon wasn't there, either.

He continued searching, including some of the abandoned houses and ranches in the territory.

McGoon wasn't hiding in any of them.

Rattled, dispirited, and exhausted, Bailey made his way back to town. His mood wasn't helped by that cursed comet hovering over Sourwood like a starving albatross. The comet had turned the sky and the atmosphere a sickly shade of yellow, casting an aura of gloom, reflecting Bailey's mood at the moment.

And Bailey's mood was soured even more when he saw the Starkwells — Jedadiah and his sons Beau and Virgil, guiding their buckboard down Main Street. Jedadiah, despite his legs being pretty much useless, was doing the driving — Virgil and Beau followed behind on horseback. The back of the wagon was loaded down with their possessions. In the back was their fat Mexican housekeeper, Lardessa, who'd been with the Starkwells since Virgil and Beau were toddlers.

Jedadiah halted the wagon when he saw Bailey approach.

"Going somewhere, Jedadiah?" Bailey asked.

"Kinda looks that way, I reckon," Jedadiah said.

"Sweet limpin' Jesus," Bailey said. "Not you, too? I thought you said the comet might pass us by."

"*Might* pass us by," Jedadiah said. "From the looks of it, though, it might not. I can't let my boys die cause of my false hope."

"Well, most folks have already skedaddled," Bailey said. "Where can you go that's safe?"

"Got me a cabin up to Wichita Falls," Jedadiah said. "I suspect we'll be needing to run off any squatters — ain't been there in a month of Sundays. We may get ambushed along the way by some drifters who like what they see in the wagon — but we got to try."

"I can't say as I blame you much," Bailey said. "I wish you and your boys Godspeed. And come back to Sourwood if it ain't in cinders."

"Damn right we will," Starkwell said.

The Starkwells had been fixtures in Sourwood for three generations.

They said their farewells. Starkwell said, "You're more'n welcome to come with us if you're of a mind to, you and Agnes Jean."

"She won't leave without her Aunt Tinky," Bailey said.

Starkwell shrugged. "Women — can't live with 'em, can't drown 'em in a stock tank."

"I'll ask her," Bailey said, knowing Agnes Jean would never leave Aunt Tinky despite their always turbulent relationship. "I need to stay, Jedadiah. Someone's got to pick up the pieces in Sourwood when —"

"Helluva world," Starkwell said. "Like a poker game. Sometimes the cards come up aces when fate deals 'em down, sometimes fate won't even hand you a pair of deuces."

As Bailey watched them ride off into the distance, he felt like crying.

■ ■ ■ ■

Earlier that day, Aunt Tinky had summoned her niece to the house. When Agnes Jean arrived, Aunt Tinky was throwing clothes into a cedar hope chest; there were four suitcases, already bulging with Lord knew what.

"Don't tell me you're leaving, too," Agnes Jean said.

"No reason to stay here and wait for doomsday," Aunt Tinky said. "Lester Winninger the widower offered to take me to El Paso, where there are relatives with whom I can stay. You'd be wise to accompany me, Agnes Jean."

"I can't," she said. "Not without Billy. My place is with him now."

Aunt Tinky reached into her handbag and handed Agnes Jean a neatly folded piece of paper.

"What's this?" Agnes Jean said.

"The deed to this house," she said. "It's yours now — if Mother Nature leaves it standing, that is."

"I'm not sure I understand," Agnes Jean said.

"You really are in love with Billy Bailey, aren't you?"

"I think you know the answer to that, Aunt Tinky."

"Does he love you back?"

"I think you know the answer to that, too," Agnes Jean said.

"Then marry him," Aunt Tinky said. "Always marry the one who loves you, little lady."

Agnes Jean wasn't sure she was hearing her aunt correctly.

"I thought you didn't care for Billy," Agnes Jean said.

"I admit it looked that way," Aunt Tinky said, "but I didn't hate him, Agnes Jean. He'll make a fine, faithful husband and a good papa to that passel of kids you'll be having. He's a good man, Aggie — just like his father was — salt of the earth. Even if Bailey Senior did allow his manhood do a lot of his thinking for him. Just be happy, Agnes Jean," she said. "Even if it's just for a day or two until that cursed rock kills us all."

Chapter 33

Bailey walked over to Henrietta Primm's house. He was giving serious thought now to sweeping up Agnes Jean and those that remained and following the Starkwells to a safe haven. If, that is, there *was* a safe haven.

He rode a little further — Sourwood was rapidly becoming a ghost town.

He spotted Joseph and Josephine Cantalupo sitting forlornly in front of their now shuttered eatery, the Spaghetti Palace. Joseph had a Winchester rifle, looked like the 1866 model, across his lap.

"Good evening, Joseph and Josephine," Bailey greeted.

"*Buona sera,* Signor Billy," Joseph said. It came out "Beelee."

Josephine added, *"Fa Brutto tempo."*

Bailey looked momentarily confused until Joseph said, "She means the weather is *pazzo,* crazy."

"The weather, she be ugly, not *pazzo,*" Josephine said, correcting her husband.

"Statti zitto," Joseph snapped back at her.

"I'm not sure what that means," Bailey said.

Josephine said, "It mean '*shut-uppa* you face.' " She looked at Joseph and added, *"Va all'inferno!"*

Bailey had a fairly good idea of what that meant — the "inferno" part anyway.

"Sei uno stupido," Josephine said to him.

"Mi hai fatta girare i coglioni!" Joseph replied.

"But would you mind telling me why you're totin' that shotgun? I mean, it ain't like there are many people left in town to shoot."

"We must protect our *ristorante,*" Joseph said.

"Protect from what?" Billy said.

"Il ladro arriveranno," Joseph said.

"He mean the thieves will come," Josephine said.

"Uccidere rubare," Joseph said.

"He mean thieves come in the night and make us dead," Josephine said.

Bailey could see there was no future in arguing with a Sicilian. He said, "Almost everyone has left or are leaving. Why aren't you?"

"We no leave," Joseph said, shaking his head. Josephine, with a shake of her head, seconded the motion.

Bailey said, "You might die, Joseph."

"Everybody die," Joseph said.

"My husband," Josephine said, "he mean we no can leave this TexasSourwood." It came out as one word.

"In Sicily," Joseph said, "we own only the clothes on our backs — even *la abitazione* — our home, is owned by the government. In Lercara Friddi, the people live in *miseria.* In America we find freedom. To live as we desire, to raise *la famiglia* as we desire so our *bambinos* no die young from digging for *zolfo.*"

"Sulfur, in American," Josephine said.

"In this *magnifico* land of Texas, we free to make our way in the world, with no evil *burocrata* taking every *centesimi* in our pockets."

"This is why we choose to remain," Josephine said. "With freedom always come *poco pericolo.*"

"He mean risk," Josephine said. "If we must perish to keep the blessings of democracy and freedom from going away, then perish we will. For America."

"There is only one America and is worth dying for," Joseph added.

"Hopefully, that will not be necessary," Bailey said, not sure he believed his own words.

"Your devotion and loyalty to your adopted country is what America is all about, and it makes us all proud," Bailey said. "But there is no shame in leaving Sourwood, not with big rock hanging over our heads. Lotta folks are heading north. You'd be wise to follow them."

"Then why you stay?" Josephine asked.

"It's my job," Bailey said. "My responsibility. Sourwood is my home."

"TexasSourwood our home, too," Josephine said. "If you stay, we stay."

Bailey had yet to learn that there was no point in arguing with a Sicilian.

"I understand," he said, "or I think I understand. May the Good Lord be with you both." before trotting away.

"Dio ti benedica!" Joseph called out.

Bailey had no idea what Joseph said but it did sound nice.

As Bailey halted to a stop in front of Miss Henrietta Primm's home, even outside he could hear Miss Esmerelda and Miss Henrietta screaming insults and worse at each other. He wasn't sure if it was the same fight or a brand new one.

"Ever'one knows your biscuit ain't done in the middle," Miss Esmerelda said.

"And if I had a dog as ugly as you," Miss Henrietta snapped back, "I'd shave his butt and make him walk backwards!"

"You're uglier than a lard bucket full of armpits," Miss Esmerelda said.

"And your face looks like a nickel's worth of dog meat," Miss Henrietta said.

"And *you're* about as popular as a rattlesnake at a square dance!" Miss Esmerelda said.

"You couldn't hold onto a man if you nailed his feet to the floor," Miss Henrietta said.

Bailey walked into the house and screamed, "*Enough,* both of y'all!"

"She started it," Miss Henrietta said.

"No, *you* did— said I was worse than hair in the butter," Miss Esmerelda said.

"No, I said you're uglier than a lard bucket full of armpits," Miss Henrietta said.

"Hobble your lips, dad-garnit," Bailey said. "Where's Agnes Jean?"

"She left to fetch my bible," Miss Esmerelda said.

"Alone?" Bailey asked, getting angrier by the minute. "You let her go alone? When?"

"A few hours ago," Miss Henrietta said. "Miss dumbhead here said the map to the buried gold was in it."

"Is it?" Bailey asked.

The front door swung open. Reverend Goodrich stepped inside. He'd been listening outside.

"Yes and no," Goodrich said. "We found it all right but there was no pot of gold at the end of the rainbow."

Miss Esmerelda started cackling. "Darn straight, you saphead. It was a fake, put there to fool the likes of y'all."

"You sent Agnes Jean out there knowing the map was a fake?" Bailey asked, giving some thought to strangling Miss Esmerelda.

"Then where is the map?" Goodrich said.

Miss Esmerelda tapped her head. "Right here, Reverend Peckerwood, right here. Always has been all this time."

"Then perhaps you'll draw me a real map," Goodrich said.

"When hell freezes over," Miss Esmerelda said.

"Oh, you'll do it," Goodrich said. "If you ever want to see that very lovely Agnes Jean again. And if not, McGoon will let his two reprobates have at her and rip little Miss Agnes Jean from gullet to gizzard. When those savages get done with her, there won't be enough left to feed a canary."

Bailey hauled off and smashed Goodrich

with everything he had, knocking the good reverend over the parlor couch. He pressed the barrel of his pistol against Goodrich's snoot.

"You stinkin' maggot," Bailey said. "Tell me where you got her or so help me, Lord, I'll paint this room with your brains."

"Go ahead, if it makes your day brighter," Goodrich said. "But if I ain't back by sundown with a map to the exact location of that gold, you best find yourself another lady friend."

"Goodness!" Miss Henrietta gasped.

"Where you gonna spend it, you miserable jackal?" Miss Esmerelda said. "In hell? From where I'm sittin', Satan got no use for gold. All he wants are wicked souls such as your ownself."

"He's welcome to mine," Goodrich said, "but only *after* the gold is in my greedy little hands."

Bailey wanted to put a bullet in Goodrich's head. But he also wanted Agnes Jean back more than he'd ever wanted anything. Goodrich was telling the truth. They'd kill Agnes Jean after having their way . . .

He pushed those thoughts out of his mind. For now.

"Do as he says, Miss Esmerelda," Bailey said. "He's got us over a barrel."

"Oh, for heaven's sake," the old gal said. "I'm blind if you hadn't taken note."

"You tell it," Goodrich said, and motioned to Miss Henrietta, "and she'll write it all down."

"You got any paper and something to write with?" Bailey asked.

Miss Henrietta rooted out both from the top drawer of her chifforobe. She said to Miss Esmerelda, "Go ahead, crazy lady."

Miss Esmerelda reached into the pocket of her apron, pulled out a pair of reading glasses, and put them on.

"Didn't you say you were blind?" Goodrich asked.

"I did and I am," she responded.

"Then what are the spectacles for?"

"They help me hear better."

"Well fine," Goodrich said. "Start talking."

"You ready, Henrietta?" Miss Esmerelda asked.

"I'll never be ready for you," she said, "but go ahead on."

"You know where my cabin is, right?"

"We know, Miss Esmerelda, we know," Bailey said.

"First then," she went on, "open the door and step outside. You writin' this down?"

Miss Henrietta said, "I will when you say

something *worth* writing down."

"All right then," Miss Esmerelda said. "Go fifty paces due east to where the two Tuddywood trees stand side by side . . ."

"How far is fifty paces?" Miss Henrietta asked.

"One pace more than forty-nine," Miss Esmerelda said.

"What I meant was," Miss Henrietta said, "one pace can be equal to three paces depending on how long your legs are. A little man can walk ten paces, but a big man can walk the same distance in two or three paces."

"Just look for the two darn Tuddywoods," Miss Esmerelda snapped.

Miss Henrietta scribbled something down.

"Then turn due north for another —"

"If your left leg is shorter," Miss Henrietta said, "you likely favor your right leg. You could end up walking in circles."

Miss Esmerelda ignored her. She repeated, "Turn due north for another —"

"You sure it's not south?" Miss Henrietta asked. "Because if you're walking due north, the sun will —"

"Due north!" Miss Esmerelda screamed. "If I meant due south, I'd say due south!"

"I thought you said due north."

"I *did* say due north, you ninny."

"Then why are you saying turn due south?"

"I *didn't* say turn due south," Miss Esmerelda said. "You did."

"Is everyone in this town dull and stupid?" Goodrich said.

He snatched the pencil and paper away from Miss Henrietta and shoved them at Bailey. "Maybe you best write this down, if you know how, that is."

"I can write," Bailey said.

"That's what I'm afraid of," Goodrich said. "You'll put it down all wrong just to trick me."

He was about to hand the paper and pencil back to Miss Henrietta but then pointed at something she'd put down.

"What are these?" he asked. "They look like flowers."

"They are flowers," Miss Henrietta said. "I don't know how to draw a Tuddywood tree."

Goodrich said to Miss Esmerelda, "Please continue." To Miss Henrietta he said, "And no more interruptions, lady."

Miss Henrietta said haughtily, "I just didn't want you to get lost."

"Thank you," Goodrich said.

Miss Esmerelda continued, "When you

get to Possum Hollow Creek, follow the trail to —"

"It hasn't been called Possum Hollow Creek in thirty years," Miss Henrietta said. "It was renamed Morgan's Creek, after Abner Morgan, who —"

Goodrich grunted in anger. "Would you kindly shut your pie hole," he said with a snarl.

"Don't pay her no mind," Miss Esmerelda said. "The old battleax don't even remember her own birthday."

"Well, aren't you a fine one to talk," Miss Henrietta said. "You can't even remember what you've tried to forget!"

"Miss Henrietta," Bailey said, "Please let Miss Esmerelda finish. Agnes Jean's life depends on it."

"What if she's already dead?"

"Then she ain't getting any fresher, is she?" Bailey said.

Miss Esmerelda went on, and this time with no interruptions, saying, "You cross Possum Hollow Creek, turn east for a hundred paces, and when you come to the fork in the trail, take the one on the left and walk another two hundred paces till you get to the southern catalpa tree. Twenty paces further along, you'll come to Tickle Tongue Rock. On the other side, you'll see a row of ‘willow weep for me’ bushes. Then walk to the fifth one.”

“And then?” Goodrich asked.

“Start digging,” Miss Esmerelda said.

“You may want to bring along a shovel,” Miss Henrietta suggested.

Goodrich snatched the directions from Miss Henrietta, saying to Miss Esmerelda, “This better be on the square, old lady.”

“It’s on the square, all right,” she replied. “Though not as square as that carbuncle you call your head.”

Goodrich was out the door in seconds, clutching the directions.

“I thought he’d never leave,” Miss Henrietta said.

“My gut tells me he has no plans to share the treasure with McGoon,” Bailey said. “Agnes Jean will die when Goodrich doesn’t show up at sunset.”

“Then go fetch Fendall and find her, blankethead,’ Miss Esmerelda said.

“Would you at least answer one question for me, Miss Esme?”

“What?” she asked.

“Why did you sit on that king’s ransom of gold all these years when you could’ve lived high on the hog?”

“Money don’t buy happiness,” she said. “After my husband passed, I did think about spending some of the money the gold would bring and buy myself a decent house, maybe a ranch. But I knew the minute I started spending, word would get out and relatives I never knew existed looking for a handout. Maybe I'd be a rich lady, but I'd be giving up my peace of mind. And you can't put any price on that, Billy — going to your slumber and waking up without a care or worry in the world. Peace of mind may be the greatest gift the Good Lord ever bestowed on His flock. Heck, Billy — you and your daddy were the only ones who never once asked me where the gold was hid."

"And if we had," he asked, "would you have told us?"

"Hell no," Miss Esme. "Just by askin', you'd have been no better than the rest of the greedy outhouse rats on God's green earth."

Chapter 34

Outside, Goodrich studied the directions. Miss Henrietta, fortunately, had nice, readable penmanship, save for the little comments she'd scrawled in the margins, such as, "He'd steal a fly from a blind spider," and "He wants to ravish me like all the others, the devil."

He'd fetch McGoon and his twin boneheads, then they'd go —

Go where? To retrieve the gold? Of course. However . . .

Goodrich never liked to share. And certainly not with prairie trash like Dexter McGoon. No, he'd dig up the gold and hightail it to Denver or maybe even San Francisco. If, however, the world didn't pan-fry into burnt biscuits first, which appeared to be a distinct possibility. The comet — that's what folks were calling it — was close, taking up an awfully large hunk of sky.

It was time to fish or cut bait.

It was now or never.

The Reverend Thornton Goodrich opted for now.

"I may get myself killed," he said to himself. "But as my daddy — he should rest in hell — used to say, 'Dying is just something we have to learn to live with.' "

Bailey trotted over to Doc Cutwater's office. The comet was bearing down now, almost close enough to touch, it seemed — and the closer it came, the more terrifying it appeared.

He walked into Doc's office. Doc wasn't there but Fendall was, walking in a circle with the help of a wooden crutch Doc had made.

Bailey said, "If you're trying to go somewhere, you're doing it wrong."

"Doc says I got to exercise my extremity so's I can walk," Fendall said.

"Extremity? Looks like a regular leg to me."

Fendall groaned with each step.

Either way it hurts," Fendall said. "Shoulda let Wolfie Dunderbeck operate on me.

"Dunderbeck left with some of the others," Bailey said. "Where's Doc?"

"Handing out bottles of that snake oil

medicine to whoever's still around. Mixed up a big batch."

Fendall picked one of the bottles off Doc's desk and was about to sip when Bailey jerked it away from him.

"Hey!" Fendall protested. "Doc give it to me. For the pain."

"Little pain never killed nobody," Bailey said. "I need you clear-headed. McGoon and his skunks kidnapped Agnes Jean."

"On the level? Where is she?"

"If I knew that," Bailey said, "I'd be out rescuing her instead of listening to you kickin' up a fuss."

"Then we best go and find her," Fendall said. "If they ain't already ripped her guts out, that is."

Bailey sighed. "You're a real joy to be around, Fendall," he said. "You know that?"

"I heard tell of it, yeah."

Agnes Jean was trying to create something edible on the old stove in the deserted ranch house McGoon was using as a hideout. It was home to an old couple, Devery and Winona Piffel. Nice, decent folks.

McGoon said, "Fix us some vittles. My belly feels like my throat's been cut."

Agnes Jean fell silent. She knew McGoon was in a bad humor — it was nearly sundown and Goodrich had yet to show his face. McGoon suspected the worst.

Agnes Jean did her best. In the pot simmering on the stove were chunks of rattlesnake, dandelions, mustard plants, wild garlic, watercress, and some rat meat.

The stew smelled like week-old socks but when Agnes Jean dished it out, the men attacked it voraciously.

Mossy and Sneed ate but weren't too pleased with Agnes Jean's vittles. Sneed Hearn made a face while Mossy asked, "What in tarnation is this slop? Tastes like a drunken jackass walked backwards through it."

"Enjoy," Agnes Jean said.

"We move at first light," McGoon said, trying to chew some chewy rattlesnake. "I think that Reverend Goodrich has gotten greedy."

"Greedrich has gotten goody," Sneed Hearn said.

"Would you shut up, Sneed," said Mossy. "What about the little lady here?"

"We can't take her," McGoon said. "So we best kill her."

"Mean we can't even have at her after supper?" Mossy asked, as though Agnes Jean wasn't even there.

"Save your Tuddy-pickin' animal urges for

another time," McGoon said. "This here is business."

"But I mean business."

"Finish your supper and get some shuteye," McGoon said. "You boys are gonna need it. We'll decide what to do with the lady in the morning."

"He never lets us have no fun," Mossy murmured to Sneed Hearn.

An hour later, Agnes Jean, tied to a chair with her arms pinned snugly and firmly behind her, was wide awake. Mortal fear overpowered any attempts at slumber.

Not so for McGoon, who'd drifted off slumped in a settee and now snored blissfully. Mossy likewise had curled up on a rug in the parlor. There were, of course, actual beds in the place but McGoon didn't want them getting *too* comfortable. The deeper they slept, the harder they were to rouse when the bullets started flying.

Only Sneed Hearn was wide awake, staring at her like he was reading a learner's manual on chicken ranching. His expression never changed and for a moment Agnes Jean wasn't sure he was even conscious.

"Mr. Hearn? Sneed?"

His expression never changed. He said, "Yes?"

"It's very chilly in here," she said.

Actually, it was hotter than blazes but Agnes Jean faked a shiver. She had no idea where Hearn was from or, for that matter, his ethnic background. Was he attracted to her in a sinful way? Maybe, but he was impossible to read — he had one expression, stoic.

She tried Spanish. "Brrr. . . . *muy frio*!"

She got no reaction on that attempt. She had a passing familiarity with other languages due to all the immigrants who came into the mercantile.

She tried German, struggling to find the right words. *"Es . . . ist . . . sehr . . . kalt . . . hier."*

Hearn said nothing, looking for all the world like an oil painting.

She tried French, even if Sneed Hearn looked about as French as a Johnny cake. *"Il fait tres froid ici."*

As a last resort, she said, "I would like to defecate in the umbrella of your sister."

For reasons she'd never completely understand, Sneed responded. "Cold you are?"

She doubted Sneed Hearn was oblivious to hot or cold weather. Still, with perhaps the only shred of chivalry he possessed, he said, "A fire then I build. Lady be not cold."

He piled very dry logs into the fireplace and struck a match. The fire roared to life instantly. Smoke went up the chimney.

Pleased with himself, Sneed Hearn tried a smile but it looked more like a grimace. His mouth looked insanely like piano keys — white where there were teeth and black where they were not.

He was very excited now and was thinking about jumping on her when McGoon snapped awake and saw the fire. He thought at first he was dreaming but the heat that engulfed the parlor struck him like a punch in the snoot.

"You started a fire, you ignoramus?" he bellowed.

"Lady ask me," Hearn said.

"Lady ask me," he said, mocking Hearn. "I'm surprised you didn't just let her go." McGoon's face was flushed the color of pickled beets.

"What?" Mossy said, awake now.

"Douse that fire, you pea brains," McGoon said, "or I'll whale the tar out of you both."

"I didn't do nothin'," Mossy protested.

"Being born, that was your first mistake," McGoon said.

Bailey and Fendall had no real idea where to look for Agnes Jean, though Billy reasoned they were likely in the general vicinity.

Bailey tried hard to not imagine the tortures of the damned the McGoon gang was inflicting on Agnes Jean — if she wasn't dead already — but they came creeping back in as he and Fendall passed now-deserted ranches. Bailey asked himself if the search was even necessary, seeing how they might all be pushing up daisies this time tomorrow. Up above, the comet continued its furious trajectory and looked like it was actually glaring at them.

They passed another small ranch which, like the others, seemed cold and deserted.

"Ain't that the Piffel spread over yonder?" Fendall asked.

"I believe so," Bailey said, not much in the mood for conversation. "Devery and his missus cleared out with the others a few days ago."

"My understanding, too," Fendall said.

It hit Bailey in the face like a giant mud ball. "So if they lit out, why is smoke coming from the chimney?"

"Good question," Fendall said.

"They're holed up in there, and ready to slaughter on anything that moves," Bailey said. "It makes some crazy kind of sense — they'd never expect us to search so close to town. What's called hiding in plain sight."

"I think you got the situation pegged, old son," Fendall said.

"You've been in tougher spots than this, Fendall," Billy said. "Got any ideas?"

"I'm studying on it," he replied. "We best lure them out if we can. Otherwise we're buzzard bait."

CHAPTER 35

Devery Piffel had built the ranch house with his own two hands back in '59. It was a sturdy log structure, with a brick chimney and a tin roof that was rusty but still kept the rain and the heat out. Behind it was a barn that was showing signs of age but did the job and kept the horses content in their stalls.

Piffel raised a few head of cattle, pigs, chickens, a goat or two, geese, ducks, and some quail, all of which had been devoured in the past few weeks.

There were windows on either side of the front door, another window in the kitchen, and one in the bedroom. The furnishings were modest; the sofa in the parlor room was frayed and sagged in the middle but the Piffels had neither the time or the money to buy a new one.

The bedroom, small but airy, also had a good-sized window.

Luring them out would have been a viable option but there was always the chance McGoon and his boys would come out blasting. Neither Bailey nor Fendall particularly liked those odds.

Fendall dropped to his knees and, clutching his rifle, belly-crawled over to the right side of the house. He stood and peered through the window.

Sure enough, there was Agnes Jean still tied to the chair. Fendall didn't see anyone else and that worried him.

Bailey crouched low and inched his way to the left side of the house. Like Fendall, he peered inside and saw Agnes Jean but no one else. Had those savages left?

Fendall was aiming his gun at the window when behind him he heard Mossy say, "Somethin' we can help you with?"

He slammed the butt of his rifle on Fendall's head and dropped him.

"No, but I can help you," Bailey said from behind Mossy and bashed him over the head with the butt of his pistol, knocking him silly.

Before Bailey could check on Fendall, and taking a brief second to gather his wits, McGoon came out of nowhere and brought the barrel of his rifle on Bailey's noggin, cold-cocking him flat.

"Lousy lawmen," McGoon grumbled.

Sneed Hearn, who couldn't bear missing out on all the fun, came charging out like a screaming banshee and knocked the barrel of his rifle over McGoon's head. The outlaw flopped face-down into the dirt and didn't stir.

Horrified at his mistake, and terrified of McGoon's penchant for killing, Hearn went to McGoon's side and started slapping his cheeks to bring him around. By this time, Fendall had roused. Hearn had his back to him. Fendall grabbed a log that had come loose from the fence and connected with the right side of Hearn's face.

To Fendall's surprise, the log, old and rotted, snapped in half. Hearn didn't even flinch. He was momentarily stunned. He leapt to his feet with the intention of ripping Fendall's face off when two pistol shots were fired, one smashing Hearn in the back of the head, blowing a fair piece of it into the dusk; the other shot tore through the vicinity of his left kidney. Astonishingly, Hearn didn't drop. He sported a look that would have chilled Satan's coffee. With his strength ebbing away, Hearn picked Fendall up by the neck and lifted him off the ground. He held Fendall over his head and hurled the old man right into the corral fence.

"Thumbich," Fendall croaked. His back felt like it was broken. Every move was a new adventure in pain.

Hearn walked two steps, growling like a rabid timber wolf. Bailey gave him another bullet in the brisket — this time Hearn still managed two more steps until he collapsed, his eyes crossed almost comically. He wasn't breathing anymore.

Mossy had retreated back into the cabin, Agnes Jean momentarily forgotten, and fired at where mere moments ago he had seen Bailey putting the blast on Sneed Hearn. Well, he'd kill Bailey's lady friend anyway so it wouldn't be a total loss. He put the barrel of his pistol to her head and cocked it.

At that instant, Bailey kicked in the door, not realizing it was already open a crack. He fell face forward onto the floor. Mossy spun around in surprise and fired, missing Bailey's head by an inch. Bailey aimed at him and fired, slamming Mossy right in the nose. The force of the shot sent him staggering backward, where he collapsed onto the settee — which Devery Piffel still owed five payments on. Mossy's blood soaked into the material — he looked almost as if he was catching forty winks except his eyes were still open.

Bailey frantically untied Agnes Jean, who said crossly, "About time you got here."

"Yeah, and the top of the mornin' to you," Bailey said.

"And here's a tap in the morning to you, too," she said, bopping him on the head with her fist. "Do you know they almost killed me?"

"Almost doesn't count," he said. "Come on, let's get out of here. Fendall's going to need our help."

He grabbed her wrist and pulled her halfway out the door. She pulled back.

"Not so fast," she said, and threw her arms around him, almost knocking the wind out of him. She kissed him passionately on the mouth.

"Happy now?" he asked.

She grabbed his wrist this time and yanked him toward the door. No sooner were they outside than a shot rang out and caught Bailey in his upper left arm. He stumbled forward and toppled to the ground. Agnes Jean let out a scream.

Dexter Octavius McGoon, pistol aimed squarely at Bailey's head, said, "Nice work, Bailey. You kilt all my boys."

"Happy to be of help," he said, waiting for

the inevitable bullet McGoon was intent on firing into Bailey's brain. Agnes Jean saw Hearn's rifle next to his body but there was no way she could make a dive for it in time to save her fiancé.

"You've been the raspberry seed under my wisdom tooth long enough, Mr. Deputy Marshal. Say your prayers, lawman."

"I'll see you in hell," Bailey said.

Somewhere off in the gathering light, a shot rang out from what sounded like an old Springfield. The lead caught McGoon square in the belly. He stood motionless, the pistol dropping from his hand. The sounds of two more shots pierced the dusk. One struck the outlaw in the neck and the other in his private parts, finishing the job. McGoon staggered and dropped a few feet from the body of Sneed Hearn.

Out of the gloom stepped Brigadier General Noah T. Blunt, 5th Texas Infantry, Retired. Sure enough, he was toting his 1861 Springfield.

"You all right there, son?" he asked.

Agnes Jean was busy wrapping Bailey's wounds with a tablecloth from the Piffle kitchen.

"I am now, thanks to you, General Blunt," Bailey said.

"*Brigadier* General Blunt to you, son."

"Right," Bailey said.

"You best see to Mr. Harper," Blunt said. "Looks like the old whippersnapper needs a little help."

Agnes Jean said to him, "Thank you from the bottom of my heart, Brigadier General Blunt. They aimed to kill us all!"

He nodded, saying, "And they would have." He said to Bailey, "Your daddy would have been right proud of you, William. Right proud. Now git — the town needs you."

With that, Brigadier General Noah Blunt disappeared back into the darkness.

Bailey got himself up. Agnes Jean was tending to Fendall, who was half in and half out of consciousness. Bailey looked back to say something but Brigadier General Noah Blunt had disappeared back into the darkness.

"What makes him so restless?" Bailey said.

Agnes Jean was helping Fendall to his feet. His head was bleeding; his breathing labored with what were likely a couple of broken ribs.

"How you doing, podna?" Bailey asked him, wincing with the pain in his shoulder.

"How the hell does it *look* like I'm doing?" Fendall was swaying from left to right. "Feel like I just got trampled by a rampaging bull. We git 'em all?"

"We did," Bailey answered. "We gotta get you back to town, have Doc Cutwater look you over."

"I suggest we all get back to town," Agnes Jean said.

Chapter 36

Doc Cutwater stood on a wooden crate in front of his office. Next to his crate was a second one filled with medicine bottles, pop bottles, canning jars of all shapes and sizes from whatever he could rummage from Chester Sturdley's mercantile.

Inside each bottle was a healthy dose — three ounces — of what Doc was now calling Professor Emeritus Cure-All Elixir of Life. In reality, a potent mixture of laudanum, spearmint tincture, cinnamon powder, and enough wood grain alcohol to poison every healthy liver in Texas.

Doc Cutwater had been stockpiling for a few years for emergencies. Sourwood's total annihilation, Doc believed, qualified.

He had darn near fifty gallons of 190-proof liquid fire he'd stashed in a secret crawlspace under the floor of the shed behind his home. The clear liquid lava was distilled by the notorious Rickett clan, a passel of inbred hillbillies from Eureka Springs, Arkansas. The Ricketts were father Bixby, mother Octavia, sons Clem Ray, Bucky Lee, and Just Plain Bubba. His parents, legend had it, ran out of second first names.

They were stark, raving mad, all of them, ready to disembowel anyone who wandered onto their property. The citizens of Sourwood were intimidated, cowed, anxious, and generally terror-stricken when it came to the Ricketts.

And with good reason. The Ricketts boys Clem Ray and Bucky Lee were strongly linked suspects in three rape-murders and one unsolved murder — of the boys' own father, Bixby. On orders from mother Octavia, when she caught Bixby and her own sister, Masie, drunkenly canoodling in the corn crib.

Those in Sourwood, who were victims of the Ricketts' mountain savagery in one form or another, refused to testify. Clem Ray and Bucky Lee walked free. But not for long.

Thing was, the Ricketts made some of the best corn liquor in Texas. And would have continued making some of the best corn liquor had the Rangers not chased them back into the hills of Arkansas.

Or so the story goes. Everyone knew the

Ricketts would get even more blood-thirsty and belligerent without Papa Bixby holding them back. The good folks in Sourwood knew it, Deputy Marshal Braddock Bailey knew it, and the Rangers knew it.

The Ricketts did indeed distill the best hooch but not good enough to keep them out of deep trouble. They scared people, harassed them on the street, stole their money, and lately in their drunken revelry had been getting way too touchy with the women around town.

Three nights later, the echo of gunshots were heard in the low-rising hills around the Ricketts place. On the morning of the fourth day, the Ricketts cabin — more like a shack — was found deserted. No sign of the Ricketts clan to be seen, and from the condition of the cabin, it was evident they'd left "like their rear ends were on fire," commented Deputy Marshal Braddock Bailey.

The Ricketts were never seen again. By anyone, anywhere.

Not long after, Doc Cutwater snuck onto the Ricketts place and helped himself to the endless jugs of corn the Ricketts had distilled and put up in the smokehouse before their hasty exit.

Hasty exit. Doc laughed mirthlessly. "Hell, they're probably buried ten feet away. Oh, those Rangers!"

Doc felt somewhat justified. He knew he wasn't a thief as thieves go. "This alcohol will be used to treat the sick, not inhaled down the gullets of every drunk in the territory."

This is what he told himself. He had no idea the effect his little concoction would have on the townsfolk. Hopefully put them all to sleep when the end came.

Bailey and Agnes Jean got Fendall squared away once again on the army cot Doc kept for his patients who were still woozy from the anesthesia.

"Sometimes I think Fendall is bulletproof," Bailey said. "If he —"

Agnes Jean grabbed his arm and said, "I want to get married, Billy."

Bailey was a little taken aback by her statement. He said, "So do I, Aggie, so do I. Maybe when —"

"No, Billy," she said. "I mean right now, right here in Doc's office. I don't want to wait any longer."

"Aggie, I don't have the ring with me, and all hell is about to break loose with that comet —"

"Billy, Billy, Billy," she said, and whispered in his ear. "I don't want to go to my reward . . . untouched."

It took a couple of seconds for Agnes Jean's request to register on Bailey's overcrowded brain.

"Here? Now?"

"You said you were a justice of the peace," Agnes Jean said. "That it was okay for you to marry people."

"So . . . you're asking me to marry . . . myself?"

"And me," she said. "Thought I'd come along for the ride."

"We need a witness —"

"Fendall's our witness."

"He's not even conscious," Bailey said, not believing they were arguing about . . . doing *it*.

"Are you gonna marry me and do your . . . your husbandly duties? And are your intentions honorable?"

"Do I have a choice?"

Looking exasperated, Agnes Jean took a piece of catgut Doc used to close up wounds and snapped off a foot's worth. She handed it to Bailey, saying, "My wedding ring. Tie it, Billy." He tried tying it around her fourth digit but the thread slipped off. "Try this one," she said, and held out her middle finger. Bailey wasn't crazy about the idea but he tied it up anyway.

"Will you marry me —" Bailey started to ask.

"You've got to make me a vow," Agnes Jean insisted.

"I don't know any vows," Bailey said. "Least, none that was fit for a clean conversation."

"Make something up," Agnes Jean said, almost hissing at him.

Bailey said, "I, William Thaddeus Bailey take you, Agnes Jean Willoughby to be my wedded spouse, to hold and to have more from today going forward, for good, for rotten, for poorer, to even more poorer, to love and to cherish till death when we do us part, according to God's holy ordinance. Before these witnesses, I hereby pledge —"

Agnes Jean elbowed him in the belly. "Don't overdo it, my love."

She made her wedding vows to Bailey, he made his to her again, this time as correctly as he could, saying, "With this string I do thee . . . I mean, with this wed I do thee ring."

"You may now kiss the bride," Agnes Jean said.

Bailey kissed his bride and said, "And by all that's legal in the state of Texas — and to all that ain't — I herewith pronounce me man and wife."

“Some joke,” Agnes Jean said.

They made their way back to the house that was now Aunt Tinky-less. Agnes Jean took him by the hand and led him up the stairs. They entered her bedroom, where she locked the door. She eased him down on the bed, then shrugged out of her dress. She stood before him, as naked as a jaybird.

“I’m all yours, Billy,” she said.

“It’s about time,” he said.

Chapter 37

Doc Cutwater had a medical degree from the prestigious College of Physicians and Surgeons in the City of New York.

He'd drifted south to Texas after the War of Northern Aggression and opened a practice in Sourwood, away from bloodshed and the misery he'd witnessed at the Battle of Shiloh.

He'd had not so much an inkling of where his true destiny lay — he had a silver tongue and a natural gift for gaining the public's trust.

He was a snake oil salesman at heart.

"Step right up, ladies and gentlemen," he greeted the crowd, though the crowd wasn't as crowded as Sourwood's crowds went. "Here it is, folks, Doc Cutwater's Magical Feel-Good Purple Bark Elixir, good for whatever ails you, guaranteed to soothe the nerves, calm the stomach, and makes you as regular quicker than you can dash to the outhouse. Free of charge, folks, free of charge — have all you want! One teaspoon of this elixir will ease you into a deep slumber, free of cares and worries. One teaspoon and tomorrow when you awaken, all of this will be over, as if it never happened."

"I'll take a bottle," said Milton Babbitt, a hand who worked with the Starkwells, had volunteered to stay behind and keep watch over whatever might remain of the family homestead. In exchange, Jedadiah Starkwell promised Babbitt a hunk of land and two hundred head of cattle. If there was anything to come back to.

"A bottle for my good friend Millard Rabbitt —" Doc said.

"That's Babbitt, Milton Babbitt."

"Milton and Babbitt are two people," Doc said. "Take two bottles, they're small."

Milton Babbitt asked, "Is everything you say about this stuff really true?"

Doc shrugged. He was feeling no pain himself. He said to Babbitt, "If you can't dazzle them with brilliance, baffle them with bullsh— with bovine droppings, son."

Everyone graciously accepted a bottle of Doc Cutwater's Magical Feel-Good Purple Bark Elixir. Some took more than one. Some took four or five. And they sucked them down like sarsaparilla.

"Let joy be unconfined!" he squealed as the very last bottle disappeared. He looked up at the comet, which would be upon them any time now. But his friends and colleagues in Sourwood would not die screaming as the flames of hell engulfed them. In fact, they would face eternity with faith and dignity and the brand of bravery Texans were known for: They'd get pie-eyed drunk out of their skulls.

Bailey sat on the edge of the bed, trying to pull his boots off. They'd gotten wet and were shrinking.

He was in his skivvies, grunting and cussing himself for buying such cut-rate boots. Agnes Jean lay patiently under the covers.

"Having some trouble there, dearest?" she asked.

He made a grunting noise and managed to yank off his left boot. In his anger he flung it across the room, where it smashed through the window onto the street.

"Really know how to show a gal a good time, William Bailey," she said.

The right one was being more stubborn than its counterpart. He sat down and gave the boot a hefty yank. It didn't budge. Agnes Jean sat up and embraced him, kissing his neck. "It doesn't matter, Billy," she said.

"What's a right boot between friends?"

They kissed passionately, their breathing quickening. Before they could go any further two rifle shots echoed from the town square followed by three pistol shots. Then there was a lot of hollering and whooping followed by more gunshots from pistols and rifles. In the heat of wanton desire, they sounded like Fourth of July firecrackers.

"Wow — I thought the fireworks came *after,*" Agnes Jean said.

Bailey bolted from the bed and hopped around on one foot, making his way to the bedroom door. He grabbed his gunbelt and his rifle, off a chair, forgetting momentarily that except for the one boot, he was stark naked.

"Put your pants on, Moby Dick!" Agnes Jean called after him.

Bailey managed to squirm into his pants and shirt while walking toward the center of town. The comet was bearing down, a mammoth burning rock followed by a white tail, stretching what looked like two miles across the dawning sky.

It wasn't so much the comet that got Bailey's attention — folks had been following its progress for a while now. It was, instead, the spectacle of the remaining townsfolk toting shotguns and pistols aimed at the comet

There was Doc Cutwater — who should have known better — aiming his pistol and firing it. Joseph and Josephine Cantalupo each had shotguns. Dunderbeck the butcher — who'd gotten out of the smokehouse by this time — was laying out the tools of his trade, including his trusty meat cleaver, knives of various sizes, a mallet, and a bone saw.

Even Miss Henrietta Primm and Miss Esmerelda were joining in on the fun. Both had rifles pointed skyward — Miss Esmerelda was firing in all directions, being blind and all. Another dozen or so intrepid Sourwoodians were also shooting at the comet. Even Fendall Harper had recovered enough to join the battle.

It was a bizarre sight — folks aiming at the sky but not shooting. Until Bailey heard the unmistakable voice of Brigadier General Noah T. Blunt booming out, "Fire at will! Fire at will!"

The folks did just that, opening up on the comet as if bullets could stop its deadly swath of destruction. It was coming up on Sourwood fast now, streaking across the sky. The early morning sky lit up so it looked like high noon.

"What the hell are you doing?" Bailey shouted.

"Thought you and Aggie were consternating your nuptials," Fendall said.

"We were, no thanks to you," Bailey said. "You can't stop that comet with bullets!"

"We are not delusional fools, William," Brigadier General Noah T. Blunt said. "Taking on an enemy, no matter how badly the odds are stacked up against you, is symbolic — your fellow Sourwoodians know mere bullets won't stop the destruction. These people have been living in paralyzing fear and torment since that comet showed up — shooting at it is bringing these people relief, even joy — look how happy they seem."

"They're all three sheets to the wind," Bailey said. "Snockered on Doc Cutwater's snake oil."

"True," Blunt said. "And with any luck, they'll all be unconscious when the end does come. The alternative is too ghastly to even think about. But do not fear death as it comes to all men."

"I ain't afraid of dying," Fendall said. "I just don't wanna be there when it happens."

"Oh, what the hell," Bailey said. He drew his pistol and fired at the sky. He had to admit it did make him feel a little better.

Chapter 38

The comet was bigger than three barns piled on top of each other. It streaked across the Sourwood sky at 5:48 AM, maybe half a mile above ground, traveling east to west at a speed no one thought even possible.

It came with a deafening roar, like an out of control freight train. Every window in town rattled and exploded out, covering Main Street with shattered glass. As it continued its trajectory, the comet started breaking up in earth's atmosphere, sending huge chunks of burning rock onto Sourwood. One dropped onto the roof of the boarding house, Bailey's home; it went up in flames.

Another massive rock crashed down on the livery stable. It too burst into flames and burned the stable down to its foundation.

"Take cover, y'all!" Bailey shouted. But where to take cover exactly was the question of the hour. Bailey heard Joseph Cantalupo scream in horror — a massive rock landed right on his and Josephine's spaghetti palace and exploded, turning the eatery into a flaming pile of rubble.

"Figlio di una cagna!" Joseph screamed in horror. *"Vai'all'inferno!"*

No one was certain what Joseph's rants meant in English but there was no time to mull it over. The comet went on its merry way past what was left of Sourwood and kept on going a good five miles past town and into the forest.

Thornton Goodrich was furiously digging a hole and was two feet deep when he struck paydirt. He'd followed the crudely drawn map and sure as rain, it was exactly where the old crow said it would be.

In the distance, it looked like the fourth of July in Sourwood. Big rocks, little rocks, rocks on fire — they were raining down all over the territory.

He'd followed the crudely drawn map and he pulled out a rusted tin box, smashed the lock with the shovel, and the box popped open. Sure enough, there was more gold than most people would see in their lifetimes, enough to live like a king in Mexico.

"Gold is where you find it," he said to

himself. "Ignorant fools actually trusted me."

There was a blinding flash in the sky directly above where Goodrich had been digging. The blast knocked him off his feet and sent his ill-gotten gold tumbling all over creation.

"Damn," Goodrich said and looked up to see a mammoth rock the size of an elephant hurtling straight down toward him. Goodrich muttered, "You go to hell, Mr. Rock!"

The hunk of comet hit the ground four yards away from where he was gathering up the gold, and exploded.

Goodrich was incinerated on the spot, turned to particles of dust in mere seconds, not enough of him left to fill a baby tooth.

Ten or fifteen miles to the west, Bailey's comet slammed into a body of water known as Canyon Lake, sending up a geyser a hundred feet high. Shock waves and concussions from the blast were felt fifty miles away and knocked the folks of Sourwood right off their feet, sending them flying backwards. The concussion from the blast turned some of the thankfully deserted ranches in the territory to dust.

"Are we dead?" Fendall asked.

"Not hardly," Bailey said witnessed a terrifying sight that would stay with him for the rest of his days. Over to the west, a gargantuan cloud of dust and gas and soil blossomed into the sky and straight up to the heavens, bigger than anything Bailey thought possible — it looked eerily like a giant mushroom and even blocked out the sun.

"That ain't something you see every day," Fendall commented.

The townsfolk were dazed, getting unsteadily to their feet.

They were awestruck by the cloud that looked like a giant mushroom. Joseph Cantalupo said, *"Dio abbia pieta delle nostre anime!"*

"I love his spaghetti," Fendall said, "but I really wish he'd learn to speak American."

"I think it means may God have mercy on our souls," Bailey said.

"How'd you know that?" Fendall asked.

"What else would you say?" Bailey noted.

In the distance they could see the forest burning out of control. The tree line was a distance from town and that would spare Sourwood from turning into one big tinderbox.

Bailey bolted down the street toward Agnes Jean's home. He'd left her all alone and he prayed she was still breathing. As it turned out, she had taken refuge in the kitchen bathtub, covering herself with a quilt. The house was a shambles but still standing.

Agnes Jean was a little dazed but otherwise in one piece.

"Aggie, mother of mercy, Aggie!" Bailey said, lifting her out of the tub.

She hugged him tightly and said, "What a rotten wedding, Bailey."

10 Bailey Street
Baileyville, Texas
Mr. Horace Livermore, Editor and Publisher
Livermore and Beedle Book Publishing
26 Maiden Lane
New York City, New York
USA
August 30, 1945

Dear Mr. Livermore,
I am in receipt of your letter dated 25 August.

To say I am disappointed that you have opted not to print up my account — the true account — of those deadly days that left Sourwood, Texas, close to smoldering ruins would be understatement. I was also not too surprised — you heartless Yankees would steal pennies off a dead man's eyes.

Your claim that "Nightmare in Sourwood" by T. Chesney Ragsdale is the only truthful account of what really happened in Sourwood is not only the bunk, most of it are fabrications or even outright lies.

As I stated in my first letter, I was just shy of ten years old when Bailey's Comet — which is what folks started calling it — first appeared in the sky. I'm not ashamed to say that my mother and dad opted to flee Sourwood before it struck. Like most folks in town, we lit out for Amarillo, where my mother had kinfolk.

Though Bailey's Comet left Sourwood in shambles, over the next year or so, the town managed to rebuild and return to what passed for normal.

Sourwood's rebirth would never have happened had it not been for William Bailey, our deputy marshal, who worked night and day supervising the reconstruction and never rested. His efforts went above and beyond. Hence, we renamed Sourwood

— a name nobody really liked — to Baileyville.

Oh, and if you were wondering if Billy Bailey and Agnes Jean ever did manage to "celebrate" their hasty marriage, you could ask their son William II, who became the law in Baileyville.

There were many others who helped rebuild the town — if you're curious as to whatever happened to them, you'll just have to read the book when it's published by your competitors.

I am enclosing a cashier's check for $3.65 to cover the postage for the return of my manuscript. There are several other New York publishers who have expressed interest in my account so I would be grateful if you could return it post haste.

I believe it was George Santayana who said, "Those who forget history are condemned to repeat it." It is my fervent hope that another Bailey's Comet doesn't put in an appearance in our lifetimes — in all the lifetimes of all our loved ones.

I don't know what the Almighty's plan really

was for our little town; in 2 Corinthians 5:7, it says, “For we live by faith, not by sight.”

There is also another proverb I can offer up in the best of faith: “Man plans, God laughs.”

Very truly yours,
Darris Bobby Ballard
10 Bailey Street
Baileyville, Texas

Postscript:
Mr. Ragsdale failed to mention that is has been determined by scientists that Bailey’s Comet was almost 6,000 feet in diameter and the chasm it left after hitting is over 1,000 feet deep and close to a mile across. The land around the chasm was burned to a crisp for five miles and is still growing back. The site has become what’s called a tourist attraction — folks flock there in droves every year and there’s even a snack bar where you can buy hot dogs, soda pop, ice cream, barbeque, and plenty of bicarbonate for those delicate Yankee bellies.

Bailey’s Chasm is quite impressive. You’d be wise to come pay a visit and have a grand old time — and even learn what *really* happened in Sourwood. Bring Mr. Chesney along if you dare.

ABOUT THE AUTHOR

Gary Goldstein is a career editor working for major publishers, most recently Kensington. He was the recipient of the Homestead Award from the WWA for his contributions to western publishing. Under his guidance, the William W. Johnstone franchise sold more than a million copies. A lifelong New Yorker, he currently resides in Manhattan.

The employees of Thorndike Press hope you have enjoyed this Large Print book. All our Thorndike Large Print titles are designed for easy reading, and all our books are made to last. Other Thorndike Press Large Print books are available at your library, through selected bookstores, or directly from us.

For information about titles, please call:
(800) 223-1244

or visit our website at:
gale.com/thorndike